Juanita deL. Somavía

THE DANGER TRAIL.

THE DANGER TRAIL

By

JAMES OLIVER CURWOOD

Author of
The Courage of Captain Plum, Etc.

WITH ILLUSTRATIONS BY
CHARLES LIVINGSTON BULL

NEW YORK
GROSSET & DUNLAP
PUBLISHERS
Made in the United States of America

The Danger Trail

CONTENTS

THE DANGER TRAIL

THE DANGER TRAIL

CHAPTER I

THE GIRL OF THE SNOWS

FOR perhaps the first time in his life Howland felt the spirit of romance, of adventure, of sympathy for the picturesque and the unknown surging through his veins. A billion stars glowed like yellow, passionless eyes in the polar cold of the skies. Behind him, white in its sinuous twisting through the snow-smothered wilderness, lay the icy Saskatchewan, with a few scattered lights visible where Prince Albert, the last outpost of civilization, came down to the river half a mile away.

But it was into the North that Howland looked. From the top of the great ridge which he had

1

climbed he gazed steadily into the white gloom which reached for a thousand miles from where he stood to the Arctic Sea. Faintly in the grim silence of the winter night there came to his ears the soft hissing sound of the aurora borealis as it played in its age-old song over the dome of the earth, and as he watched the cold flashes shooting like pale arrows through the distant sky and listened to its whispering music of unending loneliness and mystery, there came on him a strange feeling that it was beckoning to him and calling to him—telling him that up there very near to the end of the earth lay all that he had dreamed of and hoped for since he had grown old enough to begin the shaping of a destiny of his own.

He shivered as the cold nipped at his blood, and lighted a fresh cigar, half-turning to shield himself from a wind that was growing out of the east. As the match flared in the cup of his hands for an instant there came from the black gloom of the balsam and spruce at his feet a wailing, hungerful cry that brought a startled breath from his lips. It was a cry such as Indian dogs make about the tepees of masters who are newly dead. He had never heard such a cry before, and yet he knew that it was a wolf's. It impressed him with an awe which was new to him and he stood as motionless as the trees about him until, from out the gray night-gloom to the west, there came an answering cry, and then, from far to the north, still another.

"Sounds as though I'd better go back to town," he said to himself, speaking aloud. "By George, but it's lonely!"

He descended the ridge, walked rapidly over the hard crust of the snow across the Saskatchewan, and assured himself that he felt considerably easier when the lights of Prince Albert gleamed a few hundred yards ahead of him.

Jack Howland was a Chicago man, which means that he was a hustler, and not overburdened with sentiment. For fifteen of his thirty-one years he had been hustling. Since he could

3

easily remember, he had possessed to a large measure but one ambition and one hope. With a persistence which had left him peculiarly a stranger to the more frivolous and human sides of life he had worked toward the achievement of this ambition, and to-night, because that achievement was very near at hand, he was happy. He had never been happier. There flashed across his mental vision a swiftly moving picture of the fight he had made for success. It had been a magnificent fight. Without vanity he was proud of it, for fate had handicapped him at the beginning, and still he had won out. He saw himself again the homeless little farmer boy setting out from his Illinois village to take up life in a great city; as though it had all happened but yesterday he remembered how for days and weeks he had nearly starved, how he had sold papers at first, and then, by lucky chance, became errand boy in a big drafting establishment. It was there that the ambition was born in him. He saw great engineers come and go—men who were greater you are from Lac Bain. That's a good distance north, isn't it?"

"Four hundred miles," replied the factor with quiet terseness. "We're on the edge of the Barren Lands."

"Whew!" Howland shrugged his shoulders. Then he volunteered, "I'm going north myself to-morrow."

"Post man?"

"No; engineer. I'm putting through the Hudson Bay Railroad."

He spoke the words quite clearly and as they fell from his lips the half-breed, partly concealed in the gloom behind him, straightened with the alert quickness of a cat. He leaned forward eagerly, his black eyes gleaming, and then rose softly from his seat. His moccasined feet made no sound as he came up behind Howland. It was the big huskie who first gave a sign of his presence. For a moment the upturned eyes of the young engineer met those of the half-breed. That look gave Howland a glimpse of a face

9

which he could never forget—a thin, dark, sensitive face framed in shining, jet-black hair, and a pair of eyes that were the most beautiful he had ever seen in a man. Sometimes a look decides great friendship or bitter hatred between men. And something, nameless, unaccountable, passed between these two. Not until the half-breed had turned and was walking swiftly away did Howland realize that he wanted to speak to him, to grip him by the hand, to know him by name. He watched the slender form of the Northerner, as lithe and as graceful in its movement as a wild thing of the forests, until it passed from the door out into the night.

"Who was that?" he asked, turning to the factor.

"His name is Croisset. He comes from the Wholdaia country, beyond Lac la Ronge."

"French?"

"Half French, half Cree."

The factor resumed his steady gaze out into the white distance of the night, and Howland

10

gave up his effort at conversation. After a little his companion shoved back his chair and bade him good night. The Crees and Chippewayan followed him, and a few minutes later the two white hunters left the engineer alone before the windows.

"Mighty funny people," he said half aloud. "Wonder if they ever talk!"

He leaned forward, elbows on knees, his face resting in his hands, and stared to catch a sign of moving life outside. In him there was no desire for sleep. Often he had called himself a night-bird, but seldom had he been more wakeful than on this night. The elation of his triumph, of his success, had not yet worn itself down to a normal and reasoning satisfaction, and his chief longing was for the day, and the day after that, and the next day, when he would take the place of Gregson and Thorne. Every muscle in his body was vibrant in its desire for action. He looked at his watch. It was only ten o'clock. Since supper he had smoked almost ceaselessly.

11

Now he lighted another cigar and stood up close
to one of the windows.

Faintly he caught the sound of a step on the
board walk outside. It was a light, quick step,
and for an instant it hesitated, just out of his
vision. Then it approached, and suddenly the
figure of a woman stopped in front of the window. How she was dressed Howland could not
have told a moment later. All that he saw was
the face, white in the white night—a face on
which the shimmering starlight fell as it was
lifted to his gaze, beautiful, as clear-cut as a
cameo, with eyes that looked up at him half-
pleadingly, half-luringly, and lips parted, as if
about to speak to him. He stared, moveless in
his astonishment, and in another breath the face
was gone.

With a hurried exclamation he ran across the
empty room to the door and looked down the
starlit street. To go from the window to the door
took him but a few seconds, yet he found the
street deserted—deserted except for a solitary

figure three blocks away and a dog that growled at him as he thrust out his head and shoulders. He heard no sound of footsteps, no opening or closing of a door. Only there came to him that faint, hissing music of the northern skies, and once more, from the black forest beyond the Saskatchewan, the infinite sadness of the wolf-howl.

CHAPTER II

LIPS THAT SPEAK NOT

HOWLAND was not a man easily suscepti-
ble to a pair of eyes and a pretty face.
The practical side of his nature was too much
absorbed in its devices and schemes for the building of material things to allow the breaking in
of romance. At least Howland had always com-
plimented himself on this fact, and he laughed a
little nervously as he went back to his seat near
the window. He was conscious that a flush of unusual excitement had leaped into his cheeks and
already the practical side of him was ashamed of
that to which the romantic side had surrendered.

"The deuce, but she was pretty!" he excused
himself. "And those eyes—"

Suddenly he checked himself. There had been
more than the eyes; more than the pretty face!
Why had the girl paused in front of the win-

14

dow? Why had she looked at him so intently, as though on the point of speech? The smile and the flush left his face as these questions came to him and he wondered if he had failed to comprehend something which she had meant him to understand. After all, might it not have been a case of mistaken identity? For a moment she had believed that she recognized him—then, seeing her mistake, had passed swiftly down the street. Under ordinary circumstances Howland would have accepted this solution of the incident. But to-night he was in an unusual mood, and it quickly occurred to him that even if his supposition were true it did not explain the pallor in the girl's face and the strange entreaty which had glowed for an instant in her eyes.

Anyway it was none of his business, and he walked casually to the door. At the end of the street, a quarter of a mile distant, a red light burned feebly over the front of a Chinese restaurant, and in a mechanical fashion his footsteps led him in that direction.

15

"I'll drop in and have a cup of tea," he assured himself, throwing away the stub of his cigar and filling his lungs with great breaths of the cold, dry air. "Lord, but it's a glorious night! I wish Van Horn could see it."

He stopped and turned his eyes again into the North. Its myriad stars, white and unshivering, the elusive play of the mysterious lights hovering over the pole, and the black edge of the wilderness beyond the river were holding a greater and greater fascination for him. Since morning, when he had looked on that wilderness for the first time in his life, new blood had entered into him, and he rejoiced that it was this wonderful world which was to hold for him success and fortune. Never had he dreamed that the mere joy of living would appeal to him as it did now; that the act of breathing, of seeing, of looking on wonders in which his hands had taken no part in the making, would fill him with the indefinable pleasure which had suddenly become his experience. He wondered, as he still stood gazing into

16

the infinity of that other world beyond the Saskatchewan, if romance was really quite dead in him. Always he had laughed at romance. Work —the grim reality of action, of brain fighting brain, of cleverness pitted against other men's cleverness—had almost brought him to the point of regarding romance in life as a peculiar illusion of fools—and women. But he was fair in his concessions, and to-night he acknowledged that he had enjoyed the romance of what he had seen and heard. And most of all, his blood had been stirred by the beautiful face that had looked at him from out of the night.

The tuneless thrumming of a piano sounded behind him. As he passed through the low door of the restaurant a man and woman lurched past him and in their irresolute faces and leering stare he read the verification of his suspicions of the place. Through a second door he entered a large room filled with tables and chairs, and pregnant with strange odors. At one of the farther tables sat a long-queued Chinaman with his head bowed

17

in his arms. Behind a counter stood a second, as motionless as an obelisk in the half gloom of the dimly illuminated room, his evil face challenging Howland as he entered. The sound of a piano came from above and with a bold and friendly nod the young engineer mounted a pair of stairs.

"Tough joint," he muttered, falling into his old habit of communing with himself. "Hope they make good tea."

At the sound of his footsteps on the stair the playing of the piano ceased. He was surprised at what greeted him above. In startling contrast to the loathsome environment below he entered a luxuriously appointed room, heavily hung with oriental tapestries, and with half a dozen onyx tables partially concealed behind screens and gorgeously embroidered silk curtains. At one of these he seated himself and signaled for service with the tiny bell near his hand. In response there appeared a young Chinaman with close-cropped hair and attired in evening dress.

"A pot of tea," ordered Howland; and under

his breath he added, "Pretty deuced good for a wilderness town! I wonder——"

He looked about him curiously. Although it was only eleven o'clock the place appeared to be empty. Yet Howland was reasonably assured that it was not empty. He was conscious of sensing in a vague sort of way the presence of others somewhere near him. He was sure that there was a faint, acrid odor lurking above that of burned incense, and he shrugged his shoulders with conviction when he paid a dollar for his pot of tea.

"Opium, as sure as your name is Jack Howland," he said, when the waiter was gone. "I wonder again——how many pots of tea do they sell in a night?"

He sipped his own leisurely, listening with all the eagerness of the new sense of freedom which had taken possession of him. The Chinaman had scarcely disappeared when he heard footsteps on the stair. In another instant a low word of surprise almost leaped from his lips. Hesitating for a moment in the doorway, her face staring

19

straight into his own, was the girl whom he had
seen through the hotel window!

For perhaps no more than five seconds their
eyes met. Yet in that time there was painted on
his memory a picture that Howland knew he
would never forget. His was a nature, because
of the ambition imposed on it, that had never
taken more than a casual interest in the form and
feature of women. He had looked on beautiful
faces and had admired them in a cool, dispas-
sionate way, judging them—when he judged at
all—as he might have judged the more material
workmanship of his own hands. But this face
that was framed for a few brief moments in the
door reached out to him and stirred an interest
within him which was as new as it was pleasur-
able. It was a beautiful face. He knew that in
a fraction of the first second. It was not white,
as he had first seen it through the window. The
girl's cheeks were flushed. Her lips were parted,
and she was breathing quickly, as though from
the effect of climbing the stair. But it was her

eyes that sent Howland's blood a little faster through his veins. They were glorious eyes.

The girl turned from his gaze and seated herself at a table so that he caught only her profile. The change delighted him. It afforded him another view of the picture that had appeared to him in the doorway, and he could study it without being observed in the act, though he was confident that the girl knew his eyes were on her. He refilled his tiny cup with tea and smiled when he noticed that she could easily have seated herself behind one of the screens. From the flush in her cheeks his eyes traveled critically to the rich glow of the light in her shining brown hair, which swept half over her ears in thick, soft waves, caught in a heavy coil low on her neck. Then, for the first time, he noticed her dress. It puzzled him. Her turban and muff were of deep gray lynx fur. Around her shoulders was a collarette of the same material. Her hands were immaculately gloved. In every feature of her lovely face, in every point of her dress, she bore

21

the indisputable mark of refinement. The quizzical smile left his lips. The thoughts which at first had filled his mind as quickly disappeared. Who was she? Why was she here?

With cat-like quietness the young Chinaman entered between the screens and stood beside her. On a small tablet which Howland had not before observed she wrote her order. It was for tea. He noticed that she gave the waiter a dollar bill in payment and that the Chinaman returned seventy-five cents to her in change.

"Discrimination," he chuckled to himself. "Proof that she's not a stranger here, and knows the price of things."

He poured his last half cup of tea and when he lifted his eyes he was surprised to find that the girl was looking at him. For a brief interval her gaze was steady and clear; then the flush deepened in her cheeks; her long lashes drooped as the cold gray of Howland's eyes met hers in unflinching challenge, and she turned to her tea. Howland noted that the hand which lifted the little Japanese pot was trembling slightly. He leaned forward, and as if impelled by the movement, the girl turned her face to him again, the tea-urn poised above her cup. In her dark eyes was an expression which half brought him to his feet, a wistful glow, a pathetic and yet half-frightened appeal to him. He rose, his eyes questioning her, and to his unspoken inquiry her lips formed themselves into a round, red O, and she nodded to the opposite side of her table.

"I beg your pardon," he said, seating himself. "May I give you my card?"

He felt as if there was something brutally indecent in what he was doing and the knowledge of it sent a red flush to his cheeks. The girl read his name, smiled across the table at him, and with a pretty gesture, motioned him to bring his cup and share her tea with her. He returned to his table and when he came back with the cup in his hand she was writing on one of the pages of the tablet, which she passed across to him.

"You must pardon me for not talking," he

read, "I can hear you very well, but I, unfortunately, am a mute."

He could not repress the low ejaculation of astonishment that came to his lips, and as his companion lifted her cup he saw in her face again the look that had stirred him so strangely when he stood in the window of the Hotel Windsor. Howland was not a man educated in the trivialities of chance flirtations. He lacked finesse, and now he spoke boldly and to the point, the honest candor of his gray eyes shining full on the girl.

"I saw you from the hotel window to-night," he began, "and something in your face led me to believe that you were in trouble. That is why I have ventured to be so bold. I am the engineer in charge of the new Hudson Bay Railroad, just on my way to Le Pas from Chicago. I'm a stranger in town. I've never been in this—this place before. It's a very nice tea-room, an admirable blind for the opium stalls behind those walls."

In a few terse words he had covered the situation, as he would have covered a similar situation

in a business deal. He had told the girl who and
what he was, had revealed the cause of his interest in her, and at the same time had given her to
understand that he was aware of the nature of
their present environment. Closely he watched
the effect of his words and in another breath was
sorry that he had been so blunt. The girl's eyes
traveled swiftly about her; he saw the quick rise
and fall of her bosom, the swift fading of the
color in her cheeks, the affrighted glow in her
eyes as they came back big and questioning to
him.

"I didn't know," she wrote quickly, and hesitated. Her face was as white now as when Howland had looked on it through the window. Her
hand trembled nervously and for an instant her
lip quivered in a way that set Howland's heart
pounding tumultuously within him. "I am a
stranger, too," she added. "I have never been in
this place before. I came because—"

She stopped, and the catching breath in her
throat was almost a sob as she looked at How-

land. He knew that it took an effort for her to write the next words.

"I came because you came."

"Why?" he asked. His voice was low and assuring. "Tell me—why?"

He read her words as she wrote them, leaning half across the table in his eagerness.

"I am a stranger," she repeated. "I want some one to help me. Accidentally I learned who you were and made up my mind to see you at the hotel, but when I got there I was afraid to go in. Then I saw you in the window. After a little you came out and I saw you enter here. I didn't know what kind of place it was and I followed you. Won't you please go with me—to where I am staying—and I will tell you—"

She left the sentence unfinished, her eyes pleading with him. Without a word he rose and seized his hat.

"I will go, Miss—" He laughed frankly into her face, inviting her to write her name. For a moment she smiled back at him, the color bright-

ening her cheeks. Then she turned and hurried
down the stair.

Outside Howland gave her his arm. His eyes,
passing above her, caught again the luring play
of the aurora in the north. He flung back his
shoulders, drank in the fresh air, and laughed in
the buoyancy of the new life that he felt.

"It's a glorious night!" he exclaimed.

The girl nodded, and smiled up at him. Her
face was very near to his shoulder, ever more
beautiful in the white light of the stars.

They did not look behind them. Neither heard
the quiet fall of moccasined feet a dozen yards
away. Neither saw the gleaming eyes and the
thin, dark face of Jean Croisset, the half-breed,
as they walked swiftly in the direction of the
Saskatchewan.

CHAPTER III

HOWLAND was glad that for a time there was an excuse for his silence. It began to dawn on him that this was an extraordinary adventure for a man on whose shoulders rested the responsibilities of one of the greatest engineering tasks on the continent, and who was due to take a train for the seat of his operations at eight o'clock in the morning. Inwardly he was experiencing some strange emotions; outwardly he smiled as he thought of what Van Horn would say if he knew the circumstances. He looked down at his companion; saw the sheen of her hair as it rippled out from under her fur turban, studied the soft contour of her cheek and chin, without himself being observed, and noticed, incidentally, that the top of the bewitching head beside him came just about to a

28

level with his cigar which he was smoking. He wondered if he were making a fool of himself. If so, he assured himself that there was at least one compensation. This night in Prince Albert would not be so uninteresting as it had promised to be earlier in the evening.

Where the river ferry was half drawn up on the shore, its stern frozen in the ice, he paused and looked down at the girl in quiet surprise. She nodded, smiling, and motioned across the river.

"I was over there once to-night," said Howland aloud. "Didn't see any houses and heard nothing but wolves. Is that where we're going?"

Her white teeth gleamed at him and he was conscious of a warm pressure against his arm as the girl signified that they were to cross. His perplexity increased. On the farther shore the forest came down to the river's edge in a black wall of spruce and balsam. Beyond that edge of the wilderness he knew that no part of Prince Albert intruded. It was possible that across

29

from them was a squatter's cabin; and yet if this were so, and the girl was going to it, why had she told him that she was a stranger in the town? And why had she come to him for the assistance she promised to request of him instead of seeking it of those whom she knew?

He asked himself these questions without putting them in words, and not until they were climbing up the frozen bank of the stream, with the shadows of the forest growing deeper about them, did he speak again.

"You told me you were a stranger," he said, stopping his companion where the light of the stars fell on the face which she turned up to him. She smiled, and nodded affirmatively.

"You seem pretty well acquainted over here," he persisted. "Where are we going?"

This time she responded with an emphatic negative shake of her head, at the same time pointing with her free hand to the well-defined trail that wound up from the ferry landing into the forest. Earlier in the day Howland had been told that this was the Great North Trail that led into the vast wildernesses beyond the Saskatchewan. Two days before, the factor from Lac Bain, the Chippewayan and the Crees had come in over it. Its hard crust bore the marks of the sledges of Jean Croisset and the men from the Lac la Ronge country. Since the big snow, which had fallen four feet deep ten days before, a forest man had now and then used this trail on his way down to the edge of civilization; but none from Prince Albert had traveled it in the other direction. Howland had been told this at the hotel, and he shrugged his shoulders in candid bewilderment as he stared down into the girl's face. She seemed to understand his thoughts, and again her mouth rounded itself into that bewitching red O, which gave to her face an expression of tender entreaty, of pathetic grief that the soft lips were powerless to voice the words which she wished to speak. Then, suddenly, she darted a few steps from Howland and with the toe of her shoe formed a single word in

the surface of the snow. She rested her hand
lightly on Howland's shoulder as he bent over to
make it out in the elusive starlight.

"Camp!" he cried, straightening himself. "Do
you mean to say you're camping out here?"

She nodded again and again, delighted that he
understood her. There was something so child-
ishly sweet in her face, in the gladness of her
eyes, that Howland stretched out both his hands
to her, laughing aloud. "You!" he exclaimed.
"You—camping out here!" With a quick little
movement she came to him, still laughing with
her eyes and lips, and for an instant he held both
her hands tight in his own. Her lovely face was
dangerously near to him. He felt the touch of
her breath on his face, for an instant caught the
sweet scent of her hair. Never had he seen eyes
like those that glowed up at him softly, filled
with the gentle starlight; never in his life had
he dreamed of a face like this, so near to him that
it sent the blood leaping through his veins in
strange excitement. He held the hands tighter,

and the movement drew the girl closer to him, until for no more than a breath he felt her against his breast. In that moment he forgot all sense of time and place; forgot his old self—Jack Howland—practical, unromantic, master-builder of railroads; forgot everything but this presence of the girl, the warm pressure against his breast, the lure of the great brown eyes that had come so unexpectedly into his life. In another moment he had recovered himself. He drew a step back, freeing the girl's hands.

"I beg your pardon," he said softly. His cheeks burned hotly at what he had done, and turning squarely about he strode up the trail. He had not taken a dozen paces, when far ahead of him he saw the red glow of a fire. Then a hand caught his arm, clutching at it almost fiercely, and he turned to meet the girl's face, white now with a strange terror.

"What is it?" he cried. "Tell me—"

He caught her hands again, startled by the look in her eyes. Quickly she pulled herself away. A dozen feet behind her, in the thick shadows of the forest trees, something took shape and movement. In a flash Howland saw a huge form leap from the gloom and caught the gleam of an uplifted knife. There was no time for him to leap aside, no time for him to reach for the revolver which he carried in his pocket. In such a crisis one's actions are involuntary, machine-like, as if life, hovering by a thread, preserves itself in its own manner and without thought or reasoning on the part of the creature it animates.

For an instant Howland neither thought nor reasoned. Had he done so he would probably have met his mysterious assailant, pitting his naked fists against the knife. But the very mainspring of his existence—which is self-preservation—called on him to do otherwise. Before the startled cry on his lips found utterance he flung himself face downward in the snow. The move saved him, and as the other stumbled over his body, pitching headlong into the trail, he snatched forth his revolver. Before he could fire there came a roar like that of a beast from behind him and a terrific blow fell on his head. Under the weight of a second assailant he was crushed to the snow, his pistol slipped from his grasp, and two great hands choked a despairing cry from his throat. He saw a face over him, distorted with passion, a huge neck, eyes that flamed like angry garnets. He struggled to free his pinioned arms, to wrench off the death-grip at his throat, but his efforts were like those of a child against a giant. In a last terrible attempt he drew up his knees inch by inch under the weight of his enemy; it was his only chance, his only hope. Even as he felt the fingers about his throat, sinking like hot iron into his flesh, and the breath slipping from his body, he remembered this murderous knee-punch taught to him by the rough fighters of the Inland Seas, and with all the life that remained in him he sent it crushing into the other's abdomen. It was a moment before he knew that it had been successful, before the film cleared from his eyes and he

saw his assailant groveling in the snow. He rose
to his feet, dazed and staggering from the effect
of the blow on his head and the murderous grip
at his throat. Half a pistol shot down the trail
he saw indistinctly the twisting of black objects
in the snow, and as he stared one of the objects
came toward him.

"Do not fire, M'seur Howland," he heard a
voice call. "It ees I—Jean Croisset, a friend!
Blessed Saints, that was—what you call heem?—
close call?"

The half-breed's thin dark face came up smiling out of the white gloom. For a moment Howland did not see him, scarcely heard his words.
Wildly he looked about him for the girl. She
was gone.

"I happened here—just in time—with a club,"
continued Croisset. "Come, we must go."

The smile had gone from his face and there
was a commanding firmness in the grip that fell
on the young engineer's arm. Howland was conscious that things were twisting about him and

that there was a strange weakness in his limbs. Dumbly he raised his hands to his head, which hurt him until he felt as if he must cry out in his pain.

"The girl—" he gasped weakly.

Croisset's arm tightened about his waist.

"She ees gone!" Howland heard him say; and there was something in the half-breed's low voice that caused him to turn unquestioningly and stagger along beside him in the direction of Prince Albert.

And yet as he went, only half-conscious of what he was doing, and leaning more and more heavily on his companion, he knew that it was more than the girl's disappearance that he wanted to understand. For as the blow had fallen on his head he was sure that he had heard a woman's scream; and as he lay in the snow, dazed and choking, spending his last effort in his struggle for life, there had come to him, as if from an infinite distance, a woman's voice, and the words that it had uttered pounded in his tortured brain now as his head dropped weakly against Croisset's shoulder.

"*Mon Dieu*, you are killing him—killing him!"

He tried to repeat them aloud, but his voice sounded only in an incoherent murmur. Where the forest came down to the edge of the river the half-breed stopped.

"I must carry you, M'seur Howland," he said; and as he staggered out on the ice with his inanimate burden, he spoke softly to himself, "The saints preserve me, but what would the sweet Meleese say if she knew that Jean Croisset had come so near to losing the life of this M'seur le engineer? *Ce monde est plein de fous!*"

CHAPTER IV

THE WARNING

IN only a subconscious sort of way was Howland cognizant of anything more that happened that night. When he came back into a full
sense of his existence he found himself in his bed
at the hotel. A lamp was burning low on the
table. A glance showed him that the room was
empty. He raised his head and shoulders from
the pillows on which they were resting and the
movement helped to bring him at once into a
realization of what had happened. He was hurt.
There was a dull, aching pain in his head and
neck and when he raised an inquiring hand it
came in contact with a thick bandage. He wondered if he were badly hurt and sank back again
on the pillows, lying with his eyes staring at the
faint glow of the lamp. Soon there came a sound
at the door and he twisted his head, grimacing

with the pain it caused him. Jean was looking in at him.

"Ah, M'seur ees awake!" he said, seeing the wide-open eyes. He came in softly, closing the door behind him. "*Mon Dieu,* but if it had been a heavier club by the weight of a pound you would have gone into the blessed hereafter," he smiled, approaching with noiseless tread. He held a glass of water to Howland's lips.

"Is it bad, Croisset?"

"So bad that you will be in bed for a day or so, M'seur. That is all."

"Impossible!" cried the young engineer. "I must take the eight o'clock train in the morning. I must be in Le Pas—"

"It is five o'clock now," interrupted Jean softly. "Do you feel like going?"

Howland straightened himself and fell back suddenly with a sharp cry.

"The devil!" he exclaimed. After a moment he added, "There will be no other train for two days." As he raised a hand to his aching head,

40

his other closed tightly about Jean's lithe brown
fingers. "I want to thank you for what you did,
Croisset. I don't know what happened. I don't
know who they were or why they tried to kill me.
There was a girl—I was going with her—"

He dropped his hand in time to see the strange
fire that had leaped into the half-breed's eyes.
In astonishment he half lifted himself again, his
white face questioning Croisset.

"Do you know?" he whispered eagerly. "Who
was she? Why did she lead me into that ambush? Why did they attempt to kill me?"

The questions shot from him excitedly, and he
knew from what he saw in the other's face that
Croisset could have answered them. Yet from
the thin tense lips above him there came no response. With a quick movement the half-breed
drew away his hand and moved toward the door.
Half way he paused and turned.

"M'seur, I have come to you with a warning.
Do not go to Le Pas. Do not go to the big railroad camp on the Wekusko. Return into the

South." For an instant he leaned forward, his black eyes flashing, his hands clenched tightly at his sides. "Perhaps you will understand," he cried tensely, "when I tell you this warning is sent to you—by the little Meleese!"

Before Howland could recover from his surprise Croisset had passed swiftly through the door. The engineer called his name, but there came no response other then the rapidly retreating sound of the Northerner's moccasined feet. With a grumble of vexation he sank back on his pillows. The fresh excitement had set his head in a whirl again and a feverish heat mounted into his face. For a long time he lay with his eyes closed, trying to clear for himself the mystery of the preceding night. The one thought which obsessed him was that he had been duped. His lovely acquaintance of the preceding evening had ensnared him completely with her gentle smile and her winsome mouth, and he gritted his teeth grimly as he reflected how easy he had been. Deliberately she had lured him into the ambush

42

which would have proved fatal for him had it not been for Jean Croisset. And she was not a mute! He had heard her voice; when that death-grip was tightest about his throat there had come to him that terrified cry: *"Mon Dieu,* you are killing him—killing him!"

His breath came a little faster as he whispered the words to himself. They appealed to him now with a significance which he had not understood at first. He was sure that in that cry there had been real terror; almost, he fancied, as he lay with his eyes shut tight, that he could still hear the shrill note of despair in the voice. The more he tried to reason the situation, the more inexplicable grew the mystery of it all. If the girl had calmly led him into the ambush, why, in the last moment, when success seemed about to crown her duplicity, had she cried out in that agony of terror? In Howland's heated brain there came suddenly a vision of her as she stood beside him in the white trail; he felt again the thrill of her hands, the touch of her breast for a moment against his own; saw the gentle look that had come into her deep, pure eyes; the pathetic tremor of the lips which seemed bravely striving to speak to him. Was it possible that face and eyes like those could have led him into a death-trap! Despite the evidence of what had happened he found himself filled with doubt. And yet, after all, she had lied to him—for she was not a mute!

He turned over with a groan and watched the door. When Croisset returned he would insist on knowing more about the strange occurrence, for he was sure that the half-breed could clear away at least a part of the mystery. Vainly, as he watched and waited, he racked his mind to find some reason for the murderous attack on himself. Who was "the little Meleese," whom Croisset declared had sent the warning? So far as he could remember he had never known a person by that name. And yet the half-breed had uttered it as though it would carry a vital meaning to him. "Perhaps you will understand," he had said, and

Howland strove to understand, until his brain grew dizzy and a nauseous sickness overcame him.

The first light of the day was falling faintly through the window when footsteps sounded outside the door again. It was not Croisset who appeared this time, but the proprietor himself, bearing with him a tray on which there was toast and a steaming pot of coffee. He nodded and smiled as he saw Howland half sitting up.

"Bad fall you had," he greeted, drawing a small table close beside the bed. "This snow is treacherous when you're climbing among the rocks. When it caves in with you on the side of a mountain you might as well make up your mind you're going to get a good bump. Good thing Croisset was with you!"

For a few moments Howland was speechless.

"Yes—it—was—a—bad—fall," he replied at last, looking sharply at the other. "Where is Croisset?"

"Gone. He left an hour ago with his dogs.

45

Funny fellow—that Croisset! Came in yesterday from the Lac la Ronge country a hundred miles north; goes back to-day. No apparent reason for his coming, none for his going, that I can see."

"Do you know anything about him?" asked Howland a little eagerly.

"No. He comes in about once or twice a year."

The young engineer munched his toast and drank his coffee for some moments in silence. Then, casually, he asked,

"Did you ever hear of a person by the name of Meleese?"

"Meleese—Meleese—Meleese—" repeated the hotel man, running a hand through his hair. "It seems to me that the name is familiar—and yet I can't remember—" He caught himself in sudden triumph. "Ah, I have it! Two years ago I had a kitchen woman named Meleese."

Howland shrugged his shoulders.

"This was a young woman," he said.

"The Meleese we had is dead," replied the pro-

46

prietor cheerfully, rising to go. "I'll send up for your tray in half an hour or so, Mr. Howland."

Several hours later Howland crawled from his bed and bathed his head in cold water. After that he felt better, dressed himself, and went below. His head pained him considerably, but beyond that and an occasional nauseous sensation the injury he had received in the fight caused him no very great distress. He went in to dinner and by the middle of the afternoon was so much improved that he lighted his first cigar and ventured out into the bracing air for a short walk. At first it occurred to him that he might make inquiries at the Chinese restaurant regarding the identity of the girl whom he had met there, but he quickly changed his mind, and crossing the river he followed the trail which they had taken the preceding night. For a few moments he contemplated the marks of the conflict in the snow. Where he had first seen the half-breed there were blotches of blood on the crust.

"Good for Croisset!" Howland muttered; "good for Croisset. It looks as though he used a knife."

He could see where the wounded man had dragged himself up the trail, finally staggering to his feet, and with a caution which he had not exercised a few hours before Howland continued slowly between the thick forest walls, one hand clutching the butt of the revolver in his coat pocket. Where the trail twisted abruptly into the north he found the charred remains of a camp-fire in a small open, and just beyond it a number of birch toggles, which had undoubtedly been used in place of tent-stakes. With the toe of his boot he kicked among the ashes and half-burned bits of wood. There was no sign of smoke, not a living spark to give evidence that human presence had been there for many hours. There was but one conclusion to make; soon after their unsuccessful attempt on his life his strange assailants had broken camp and fled. With them, in all probability, had gone the girl whose soft

eyes and sweet face had lured him within their
reach.

But where had they gone?

Carefully he examined the abandoned camp.
In the hard crust were the imprints of dogs'
claws. In several places he found the faint, broad
impression made by a toboggan. The marks at
least cleared away the mystery of their disappearance. Sometime during the night they had
fled by dog-sledge into the North.

He was tired when he returned to the hotel and
it was rather with a sense of disappointment than
pleasure that he learned the work-train was to
leave for Le Pas late that night instead of the
next day. After a quiet hour's rest in his room,
however, his old enthusiasm returned to him. He
found himself feverishly anxious to reach Le Pas
and the big camp on the Wekusko. Croisset's
warning for him to turn back into the South, instead of deterring him, urged him on. He was
born a fighter. It was by fighting that he had
forced his way round by round up the ladder of

success. And now the fact that his life was in danger, that some mysterious peril awaited him in the depths of the wilderness, but added a new and thrilling fascination to the tremendous task which was ahead of him. He wondered if this same peril had beset Gregson and Thorne, and if it was the cause of their failure, of their anxiety to return to civilization. He assured himself that he would know when he met them at Le Pas. He would discover more when he became a part of the camp on the Wekusko; that is, if the half-breed's warning held any significance at all, and he believed that it did. Anyway, he would prepare for developments. So he went to a gunshop, bought a long-barreled six-shooter and a holster, and added to it a hunting-knife like that he had seen carried by Croisset.

It was near midnight when he boarded the work-train and dawn was just beginning to break over the wilderness when it stopped at Etomami, from which point he was to travel by hand-car over the sixty miles of new road that had been constructed as far north as Le Pas. For three days the car had been waiting for the new chief of the road, but neither Gregson nor Thorne was with it.

"Mr. Gregson is waiting for you at Le Pas," said one of the men who had come with it. "Thorne is at Wekusko."

For the first time in his life Howland now plunged into the heart of the wilderness, and as mile after mile slipped behind them and he sped deeper into the peopleless desolation of ice and snow and forest his blood leaped in swift excitement, in the new joy of life which he was finding up here under the far northern skies. Seated on the front of the car, with the four men pumping behind him, he drank in the wild beauties of the forests and swamps through which they slipped, his eyes constantly on the alert for signs of the big game which his companions told him was on all sides of them.

Everywhere about them lay white winter. The rocks, the trees, and the great ridges, which in

this north country are called mountains, were
covered with four feet of snow and on it the sun
shone with dazzling brilliancy. But it was not
until a long grade brought them to the top of
one of these ridges and Howland looked into the
north that he saw the wilderness in all of its
grandeur. As the car stopped he sprang to his
feet with a joyous cry, his face aflame with what
he saw ahead of him. Stretching away under his
eyes, mile after mile, was the vast white desolation that reached to Hudson Bay. In speechless
wonder he gazed down on the unblazed forests,
saw plains and hills unfold themselves as his
vision gained distance, followed a frozen river
until it was lost in the bewildering picture, and
let his eyes rest here and there on the glistening,
snow-smothered bosoms of lakes, rimmed in by
walls of black forest. This was not the wilderness as he had expected it to be, nor as he had
often read of it in books. It was not the wilderness that Gregson and Thorne had described in
their letters. It was beautiful! It was magnifi-

cent! His heart throbbed with pleasure as he gazed down on it, the flush grew deeper in his face, and he seemed hardly to breathe in his tense interest.

One of the four on the car was an old Indian and it was he, strangely enough, who broke the silence. He had seen the look in Howland's face, and he spoke softly, close to his ear, "Twent' t'ousand moose down there—twent' t'ousand caribou-oo! No man—no house—more twent' t'ousand miles!"

Howland, even quivering in his new emotion, looked into the old warrior's eyes, filled with the curious, thrilling gleam of the spirit which was stirring within himself. Then again he stared straight out into the unending distance as though his vision would penetrate far beyond the last of that visible desolation—on and on, even to the grim and uttermost fastnesses of Hudson Bay; and as he looked he knew that in these moments there had been born in him a new spirit, a new being; that no longer was he the old Jack Howland whose world had been confined by office walls and into whose conception of life there had seldom entered things other than those which led directly toward the achievement of his ambitions.

The short northern day was nearing an end when once more they saw the broad Saskatchewan twisting through a plain below them, and on its southern shore the few log buildings of Le Pas hemmed in on three sides by the black forests of balsam and spruce. Lights were burning in the cabins and in the Hudson Bay Post's store when the car was brought to a halt half a hundred paces from a squat, log-built structure, which was more brilliantly illuminated than any of the others.

"That's the hotel," said one of the men. "Gregson's there."

A tall, fur-clad figure hurried forth to meet Howland as he walked briskly across the open. It was Gregson. As the two men gripped hands the young engineer stared at the other in astonishment. This was not the Gregson he had known in the Chicago office, round-faced, full of life, as active as a cricket.

"Never so glad to see any one in my life, Howland!" he cried, shaking the other's hand again and again. "Another month and I'd be dead. Isn't this a hell of a country?"

"I'm falling more in love with it at every breath, Gregson. What's the matter? Have you been sick?"

Gregson laughed as they turned toward the lighted building. It was a short, nervous laugh, and with it he gave a curious sidewise glance at his companion's face.

"Sick?—yes, sick of the job! If the old man hadn't sent us relief Thorne and I would have thrown up the whole thing in another four weeks. I'll warrant you'll get your everlasting fill of log shanties and half-breeds and moose meat and this infernal snow and ice before spring comes. But I don't want to discourage you."

"Can't discourage me!" laughed Howland

cheerfully. "You know I never cared much for theaters and girls," he added slyly, giving Gregson a good-natured nudge. "How about 'em up here?"

"Nothing—not a cursed thing." Suddenly his eyes lighted up. "By George, Howland, but I *did* see the prettiest girl I ever laid my eyes on to-day! I'd give a box of pure Havanas—and we haven't had one for a month!—if I could know who she is!"

They had entered through the low door of the log boarding-house and Gregson was throwing off his heavy coat.

"A tall girl, with a fur hat and muff?" queried Howland eagerly.

"Nothing of the sort. She was a typical Northerner if there ever was one—straight as a birch, dressed in fur cap and coat, short caribou skin skirt and moccasins, and with a braid hanging down her back as long as my arm. Lord, but she was pretty!"

"Isn't there a girl somewhere up around our camp named Meleese?" asked Howland casually.

"Never heard of her," said Gregson.

"Or a man named Croisset?"

"Never heard of him."

"The deuce, but you're interesting," laughed the young engineer, sniffing at the odors of cooking supper. "I'm as hungry as a bear!"

From outside there came the sharp cracking of a sledge-driver's whip and Gregson went to one of the small windows looking out upon the clearing. In another instant he sprang toward the door, crying out to Howland,

"By the god of love, there she is, old man! Quick, if you want to get a glimpse of her!"

He flung the door open and Howland hurried to his side. There came another crack of the whip, a loud shout, and a sledge drawn by six dogs sped past them into the gathering gloom of the early night.

From Howland's lips, too, there fell a sudden cry; for one of the two faces that were turned toward him for an instant was that of Croisset, and the other—white and staring as he had seen it that first night in Prince Albert—was the face of the beautiful girl who had lured him into the ambush on the Great North Trail!

CHAPTER V

FOR a moment after the swift passing of the sledge it was on Howland's lips to shout Croisset's name; as he thrust Gregson aside and leaped out into the night he was impelled with a desire to give chase, to overtake in some way the two people who, within the space of forty-eight hours, had become so mysteriously associated with his own life, and who were now escaping him again.

It was Gregson who recalled him to his senses.

"I thought you didn't care for theaters—*and girls*, Howland," he exclaimed banteringly, repeating Howland's words of a few minutes before. "A pretty face affects you a little differently up here, eh? Well, after you've been in this fag-end of the universe for a month or so you'll learn—"

Howland interrupted him sharply.

"Did you ever see either of them before, Greg-son?"

"Never until to-day. But there's hope, old man. Surely we can find some one in the place who knows them. Wouldn't it be jolly good fun if Jack Howland, Esquire, who has never been interested in theaters and girls, should come up into these God-forsaken regions and develop a case of love at first sight? By the Great North Trail, I tell you it may not be as uninteresting for you as it has been for Thorne and me! If I had only seen her sooner—"

"Shut up!" growled Howland, betraying irritability for the first time. "Let's go in to supper."

"Good. And I move that we investigate these people while we are smoking our after-supper cigars. It will pass our time away, at least."

"Your taste is good, Gregson," said Howland, recovering his good-humor as they seated themselves at one of the rough board tables in the dining-room. Inwardly he was convinced it would be best to keep to himself the incidents of the past two days and nights. "It was a beautiful face."

"And the eyes!" added Gregson, his own gleaming with enthusiasm. "She looked at me squarely this afternoon when she and that dark fellow passed, and I swear they're the most beautiful eyes I ever saw. And her hair——"

"Do you think that she knew you?" asked Howland quietly.

Gregson hunched his shoulders.

"How the deuce could she know me?"

"Then why did she look at you so 'squarely?' Trying to flirt, do you suppose?"

Surprise shot into Gregson's face.

"By thunder, no, she wasn't flirting!" he exclaimed. "I'd stake my life on that. A man never got a clearer, more sinless look than she gave me, and yet—— Why, deuce take it, she *stared* at me! I didn't see her again after that, but the dark fellow was in here half of the afternoon, and now that I come to think of it he did show some interest in me. Why do you ask?"

"Just curiosity," replied Howland. "I don't like flirts."

"Neither do I," said Gregson musingly. Their supper came on and they conversed but little until its end. Howland had watched his companion closely and was satisfied that he knew nothing of Croisset or the girl. The fact puzzled him more than ever. How Gregson and Thorne, two of the best engineers in the country, could voluntarily surrender a task like the building of the Hudson Bay Railroad simply because they were "tired of the country" was more than he could understand.

It was not until they were about to leave the table that Howland's eyes accidentally fell on Gregson's left hand. He gave an exclamation of astonishment when he saw that the little finger was missing. Gregson jerked the hand to his side.

"A little accident," he explained. "You'll meet 'em up here, Howland."

Before he could move, the young engineer had caught his arm and was looking closely at the hand.

"A curious wound," he remarked, without looking up. "Funny I didn't notice it before. Your finger was cut off lengthwise, and here's the scar running half way to your wrist. How did you do it?"

He dropped the hand in time to see a nervous flush in the other's face.

"Why—er—fact is, Howland, it was shot off several months ago—in an accident, of course." He hurried through the door, continuing to speak over his shoulder as he went, "Now for those after-supper cigars and our investigation."

As they passed from the dining-room into that part of the inn which was half bar and half lounging-room, already filled with smoke and a dozen or so picturesque citizens of Le Pas, the rough-jowled proprietor of the place motioned to Howland and held out a letter.

63

"This came while you was at supper, Mr. Howland," he explained.

The engineer gave an inward start when he saw the writing on the envelope, and as he tore it open he turned so that Gregson could see neither his face nor the slip of paper which he drew forth. There was no name at the bottom of what he read. It was not necessary, for a glance had told him that the writing was that of the girl whose face he had seen again that night; and her words to him this time, despite his caution, drew a low whistle from his lips.

"Forgive me for what I have done," the note ran. "Believe me now. Your life is in danger and you must go back to Etomami to-morrow. If you go to the Wekusko camp you will not live to come back."

"The devil!" he exclaimed.

"What's that?" asked Gregson, edging around him curiously.

Howland crushed the note in his hand and thrust it into one of his pockets.

"A little private affair," he laughed. "Come, Gregson, let's see what we can discover."

In the gloom outside one of his hands slipped under his coat and rested on the butt of his revolver. Until ten o'clock they mixed casually among the populace of Le Pas. Half a hundred people had seen Croisset and his beautiful companion, but no one knew anything about them. They had come that forenoon on a sledge, had eaten their dinner and supper at the cabin of a Scotch tie-cutter named MacDonald, and had left on a sledge.

"She was the sweetest thing I ever saw," exclaimed Mrs. MacDonald rapturously. "Only she couldn't talk. Two or three times she wrote things to me on a slip of paper."

"Couldn't talk!" repeated Gregson, as the two men walked leisurely back to the boarding-house. "What the deuce do you suppose that means, Jack?"

"I'm not supposing," replied Howland indifferently. "We've had enough of this pretty face, Gregson. I'm going to bed. What time do we start in the morning?"

"As soon as we've had breakfast—if you're anxious."

"I am. Good night."

Howland went to his room, but it was not to sleep. For hours he sat wide-awake, smoking cigar after cigar, and thinking. One by one he went over the bewildering incidents of the past two days. At first they had stirred his blood with a certain exhilaration—a spice of excitement which was not at all unpleasant; but with this excitement there was now a peculiar sense of oppression. The attempt that had already been made on his life together with the persistent warnings for him to return into the South began to have their effect. But Howland was not a man to surrender to his fears, if they could be called fears. He was satisfied that a mysterious peril of some kind awaited him at the camp on the Wekusko, but he gave up trying to fathom the reason for this peril, accepting in his businesslike

66

way the fact that it did exist, and that in a short time it would probably explain itself. The one puzzling factor which he could not drive out of his thoughts was the girl. Her sweet face haunted him. At every turn he saw it—now over the table in the opium den, now in the white starlight of the trail, again as it had looked at him for an instant from the sledge. Vainly he strove to discover for himself the lurking of sin in the pure eyes that had seemed to plead for his friendship, in the soft lips that had lied to him because of their silence. "Please forgive me for what I have done—" He unfolded the crumpled note and read the words again and again. "Believe me now—" She knew that he knew that she had lied to him, that she had lured him into the danger from which she now wished to save him. His cheeks burned. If a thousand perils threatened him on the Wekusko he would still go. He would meet the girl again. Despite his strongest efforts he found it impossible to destroy the vision of her beautiful face. The eyes, soft with

67

appeal; the red mouth, quivering, and with lips parted as if about to speak to him; the head as he had looked down on it with its glory of shining hair—all had burned themselves on his soul in a picture too deep to be eradicated. If the wilderness was interesting to him before it was doubly so now because that face was a part of it, because the secret of its life, of the misery that it had half confessed to him, was hidden somewhere out in the black mystery of the spruce and balsam forests.

He went to bed, but it was a long time before he fell asleep. It seemed to him that he had scarcely closed his eyes when a pounding on the door aroused him and he awoke to find the early light of dawn creeping through the narrow window of his room. A few minutes later he joined Gregson, who was ready for breakfast.

"The sledge and dogs are waiting," he greeted. As they seated themselves at the table he added, "I've changed my mind since last night, Howland. I'm not going back with you.

It's absolutely unnecessary, for Thorne can put
you on to everything at the camp, and I'd rather
lose six months' salary than take that sledge ride
again. You won't mind, will you?"

Howland hunched his shoulders.

"To be honest, Gregson, I don't believe you'd
be particularly cheerful company. What sort of
fellow is the driver?"

"We call him Jackpine—a Cree Indian—and
he's the one faithful slave of Thorne and myself
at Wekusko. Hunts for us, cooks for us, and
watches after things generally. You'll like him
all right."

Howland did. When they went out to the
sledge after their breakfast he gave Jackpine a
hearty grip of the hand and the Cree's dark face
lighted up with something like pleasure when he
saw the enthusiasm in the young engineer's eyes.
When the moment for parting came Gregson
pulled his companion a little to one side. His
eyes shifted nervously and Howland saw that he
was making a strong effort to assume an indif-

69

ference which was not at all Gregson's natural self.

"Just a word, Howland," he said. "You know this is a pretty rough country up here—some tough people in it, who wouldn't mind cutting a man's throat or sending a bullet through him for a good team of dogs and a rifle. I'm just telling you this so you'll be on your guard. Have Jackpine watch your camp nights."

He spoke in a low voice and cut himself short when the Indian approached. Howland seated himself in the middle of the six-foot toboggan, waved his hand to Gregson, then with a wild halloo and a snapping of his long caribou-gut whip Jackpine started his dogs on a trot down the street, running close beside the sledge. Howland had lighted a cigar, and leaning back in a soft mass of furs began to enjoy his new experience hugely. Day was just fairly breaking over the forests when they turned into the white trail, already beaten hard by the passing of many dogs and sledges, that led from Le Pas for a hundred miles to the camp on the Wekusko. As they struck the trail the dogs strained harder at their traces, with Jackpine's whip curling and snapping over their backs until they were leaping swiftly and with unbroken rhythm of motion over the snow. Then the Cree gathered in his whip and ran close to the leader's flank, his moccasined feet taking the short, quick, light steps of the trained forest runner, his chest thrown a little out, his eyes on the twisting trail ahead. It was a glorious ride, and in the exhilaration of it Howland forgot to smoke the cigar that he held between his fingers. His blood thrilled to the tireless effort of the grayish-yellow pack of magnificent brutes ahead of him; he watched the muscular play of their backs and legs, the eager out-reaching of their wolfish heads, their half-gaping jaws, and from them he looked at Jackpine. There was no effort in his running. His black hair swept back from the gray of his cap; like the dogs there was music in his movement, the beauty of strength, of endurance, of manhood

71

born to the forests, and when the dogs finally stop ped at the foot of a huge ridge, panting and half exhausted, Howland quickly leaped from the sledge and for the first time spoke to the Indian.

"That was glorious, Jackpine!" he cried. "But, good Lord, man, you'll kill the dogs!"

Jackpine grinned.

"They go sixt' mile in day lak dat," he grinned.

"Sixty miles!"

In his admiration for the wolfish looking beasts that were carrying him through the wilderness Howland put out a hand to stroke one of them on the head. With a warning cry the Indian jerked him back just as the dog snapped fiercely at the extended hand.

"No touch huskie!" he exclaimed. "Heem half wolf—half dog—work hard but no lak to be touch!"

"Wow!" exclaimed Howland. "And they're the sweetest looking pups I ever laid eyes on. I'm certainly running up against some strange things in this country!"

He was dead tired when night came. And yet never in all his life had he enjoyed a day so much as this one. Twenty times he had joined Jackpine in running beside the sledge. In their intervals of rest he had even learned to snap the thirty-foot caribou-gut lash of the dog-whip. He had asked a hundred questions, had insisted on Jackpine's smoking a cigar at every stop, and had been so happy and so altogether companionable that half of the Cree's hereditary reticence had been swept away before his unbounded enthusiasm. He helped to build their balsam shelter for the night, ate a huge supper of moose meat, hot-stone biscuits, beans and coffee, and then, just as he had stretched himself out in his furs for the night, he remembered Gregson's warning. He sat up and called to Jackpine, who was putting a fresh log on the big fire in front of the shelter.

"Gregson told me to be sure and have the

camp guarded at night, Jackpine. What do you think about it?"

The Indian turned with a queer chuckle, his leathery face wrinkled in a grin.

"Gregson—heem ver' much 'fraid," he replied. "No bad man here—all down there and in camp. We kep' watch evr' night. Heem 'fraid—I guess so, mebby."

"Afraid of what?"

For a moment Jackpine was silent, half bending over the fire. Then he held out his left hand, with the little finger doubled out of sight, and pointed to it with his other hand.

"Mebby heem finger ax'dent—mebby not," he said.

A dozen eager questions brought no further suggestions from Jackpine. In fact, no sooner had the words fallen from his driver's lips than Howland saw that the Indian was sorry he had spoken them. What he had said strengthened the conviction which was slowly growing within him. He had wondered at Gregson's

74

strange demeanor, his evident anxiety to get out of the country, and lastly at his desire not to return to the camp on the Wekusko with him. There was but one solution that came to him. In some way which he could not fathom Gregson was associated with the mystery which enveloped him, and adding the senior engineer's nervousness to the significance of Jackpine's words he was confident that the missing finger had become a factor in the enigma. How should he find Thorne? Surely he would give him an explanation—if there was an explanation to give. Or was it possible that they would leave him without warning to face a situation which was driving them back to civilization?

He went to sleep, giving no further thought to the guarding of the camp. A piping hot breakfast was ready when Jackpine awakened him, and once more the exhilarating excitement of their swift race through the forests relieved him of the uncomfortable mental tension under which he began to find himself. During the whole of the day Jackpine urged the dogs almost to the limit of their endurance, and early in the afternoon assured his companion that they would reach the Wekusko by nightfall. It was already dark when they came out of the forest into a broad stretch of cutting beyond which Howland caught the glimmer of scattered lights. At the farther edge of the clearing the Cree brought his dogs to a halt close to a large log-built cabin half sheltered among the trees. It was situated several hundred yards from the nearest of the lights ahead, and the unbroken snow about it showed that it had not been used as a habitation for some time. Jackpine drew a key from his pocket and without a word unlocked and swung open the heavy door.

Damp, cold air swept into the faces of the two as they stood for a moment peering into the gloom. Howland could hear the Cree chuckling in his inimitable way as he struck a match, and as a big hanging oil lamp flared slowly into light he turned a grinning face to the engineer.

"Gregson um Thorne—heem mak' thees cabin when first kam to camp," he said softly. "No be near much noise—fine place in woods where be quiet nights. Live here time—then Gregson um Thorne go live in camp. Say too far 'way from man. But that not so. Thorne 'fraid—Gregson 'fraid—"

He hunched his shoulders again as he opened the door of the big box stove which stood in the room.

Howland asked no questions, but stared about him. Everywhere he saw evidences of the taste and one-time tenancies of the two senior engineers. Heavy bear rugs lay on the board floor; the log walls, hewn almost to polished smoothness, were hung with half a dozen pictures; in one corner was a bookcase still filled with books, in another a lounge covered with furs, and in this side of the room was a door which Howland supposed must open into the sleeping apartment. A fire was roaring in the big stove before he finished his inspection and as he squared his shivering

77

back to the heat he pulled out his pipe and smiled cheerfully at Jackpine.

"Afraid, eh? And am I to stay here?"

"Gregson um Thorne say yes."

"Well, Jackpine, you just hustle over to the camp and tell Thorne I'm here, will you?"

For a moment the Indian hesitated, then went out and closed the door after him.

"Afraid!" exclaimed Howland when he had gone. "Now what the devil are they afraid of? It's deuced queer, Gregson—and ditto, Thorne. If you're not the cowards I'm half believing you to be you won't leave me in the dark to face something from which you are running away."

He lighted a small lamp and opened the door leading into the other room. It was, as he had surmised, the sleeping chamber. The bed, a single chair and a mirror and stand were its sole furnishing.

Returning to the larger room, he threw off his coat and hat and seated himself comfortably before the fire. Ten minutes later the door opened again and Jackpine entered. He was supporting another figure by the arm, and as Howland stared into the bloodless face of the man who came with him, he could not repress the exclamation of astonishment which rose to his lips. Three months before he had last seen Thorne in Chicago; a man in the prime of life, powerfully built, as straight as a tree, the most efficient and highest paid man in the company's employ. How often had he envied Thorne! For years he had been his ideal of a great engineer. And now——

He stood speechless. Slowly, as if the movement gave him pain, Thorne slipped off the great fur coat from about his shoulders. One of his arms was suspended in a sling. His huge shoulders were bent, his eyes wild and haggard. The smile that came to his lips as he held out a hand to Howland gave to his death-white face an appearance even more ghastly.

"Hello, Jack!" he greeted. "What's the matter, man? Do I look like a ghost?"

"What is the matter, Thorne? I found Gregson half dying at Le Pas, and now you—"

"It's a wonder you're not reading my name on a little board slab instead of seeing yours truly in flesh and blood, Jack," laughed Thorne nervously. "A ton of rock, man—a ton of rock, and I was under it!"

Over Thorne's shoulder the young engineer caught a glimpse of the Cree's face. A dark flash had shot into his eyes. His teeth gleamed for an instant between his tense lips in something that might have been a sneer.

Thorne sat down, rubbing his hands before the fire.

"We've been unfortunate, Jack," he said slowly. "Gregson and I have had the worst kind of luck since the day we struck this camp, and we're no longer fit for the job. It will take us six months to get on our feet again. You'll find everything here in good condition. The line is blazed straight to the bay; we've got three hundred good men, plenty of supplies, and so far as I know you'll not find a disaffected hand on the Wekusko. Probably Gregson and I will take hold of the Le Pas end of the line in the spring. It's certainly up to you to build the roadway to the bay."

"I'm sorry things have gone badly," replied Howland. He leaned forward until his face was close to his companion's. "Thorne, is there a man up here named Croisset—or a girl called Meleese?"

He watched the senior engineer closely. Nothing to confirm his suspicions came into Thorne's face. Thorne looked up, a little surprised at the tone of the other's voice.

"Not that I know of, Jack. There may be a man named Croisset among our three hundred workers—you can tell by looking at the pay-roll. There are fifteen or twenty married men among us and they have families. Gregson knows more about the girls than I. Anything particular?"

"Just a word I've got for them—if they're

here," replied Howland carelessly. "Are these my quarters?"

"If you like them. When I got hurt we moved up among the men. Brought us into closer touch with the working end, you know."

"You and Gregson must have been laid up at about the same time," said the young engineer. "That was a painful wound of Gregson's. I wonder who the deuce it was who shot him? Funny that a man like Gregson should have an enemy!"

Thorne sat up with a jerk. There came the rattle of a pan from the stove, and Howland turned his head in time to see Jackpine staring at him as though he had exploded a mine under his feet.

"Who shot him?" gasped the senior engineer. "Why—er—didn't Gregson tell you that it was an accident?"

"Why should he lie, Thorne?"

A faint flush swept into the other's pallid face. For a moment there was a penetrating glare in his eyes as he looked at Howland. Jack-pine still stood silent and motionless beside the stove.

"He told me that it was an accident," said Thorne at last.

"Funny," was all that Howland said, turning to the Indian as though the matter was of no importance. "Ah, Jackpine, I'm glad to see the coffee-pot on. I've got a box of the blackest and mildest Porto Ricans you ever laid eyes on in my kit, Thorne, and we'll open 'em up for a good smoke after supper. Hello, why have you got boards nailed over that window?"

For the first time Howland noticed that the thin muslin curtain, which he thought had screened a window, concealed, in place of a window, a carefully fitted barricade of plank. A sudden thrill shot through him as he rose to examine it. With his back toward Thorne he said, half laughing, "Perhaps Gregson was afraid that the fellow who clipped off his finger would get him through the window, eh?"

83

He pretended not to perceive the effect of his words on the senior engineer. The two sat down to supper and for an hour after they had finished they smoked and talked on the business of the camp. It was ten o'clock when Thorne and Jack-pine left the cabin.

No sooner had they gone than Howland closed and barred the door, lighted another cigar, and began pacing rapidly up and down the room. Already there were developments. Gregson had lied to him about his finger. Thorne had lied to him about his own injuries, whatever they were. He was certain of these two things—and of more. The two senior engineers were not leaving the Wekusko because of mere dissatisfaction with the work and country. They were fleeing. And for some reason they were keeping from him the real motive for their flight. Was it possible that they were deliberately sacrificing him in order to save themselves? He could not bring himself to believe this, notwithstanding the evidence against them. Both were men of irreproachable honor.

84

Thorne, especially, was a man of indomitable nerve—a man who would be the last in the world to prove treacherous to a business associate or a friend. He was sure that neither of them knew of Croisset or of the beautiful girl whom he had met at Prince Albert, which led him to believe that there were other characters in the strange plot in which he had become involved besides those whom he had encountered on the Great North Trail. Again he examined the barricaded window and he was more than ever convinced that his chance hit at Thorne had struck true.

He was tired from his long day's travel but little inclination to sleep came to him, and stretching himself out on the lounge with his head and shoulders bolstered up with furs, he continued to smoke and think. He was surprised when a little clock tinkled the hour of eleven. He had not seen the clock before. Now he listened to the faint monotonous ticking it made close to his head until he felt an impelling drowsiness creeping over him and he closed his eyes. He was almost asleep when it struck again—softly, and yet with sufficient loudness to arouse him. It had struck twelve.

With an effort Howland overcame his drowsiness and dragged himself to a sitting posture, knowing that he should undress and go to bed. The lamp was still burning brightly and he arose to turn down the wick. Suddenly he stopped. To his dulled senses there came distinctly the sound of a knock at the door. For a few moments he waited, silent and motionless. It came again, louder than before, and yet in it there was something of caution. It was not the heavy tattoo of one who had come to awaken him on a matter of business.

Who could be his midnight visitor? Softly Howland went back to his heavy coat and slipped his small revolver into his hip pocket. The knock came again. Then he walked to the door, shot back the bolt, and, with his right hand gripping the butt of his pistol, flung it wide open.

HOWLAND'S MIDNIGHT VISITOR

For a moment he stood transfixed, staring speechlessly at a white, startled face lighted up by the glow of the oil lamp. Bewildered to the point of dumbness, he backed slowly, holding the door open, and there entered the one person in all the world whom he wished most to see—she who had become so strangely a part of his life since that first night at Prince Albert, and whose sweet face was holding a deeper meaning for him with every hour that he lived. He closed the door and turned, still without speaking; and, impelled by a sudden spirit that sent the blood thrilling through his veins, he held out both hands to the girl for whom he now knew that he was willing to face all of the perils that might await him between civilization and the bay.

CHAPTER VI

THE LOVE OF A MAN

FOR a moment the girl hesitated, her ungloved hands clenched on her breast, her bloodless face tense with a strange grief, as she saw the outstretched arms of the man whom her treachery had almost lured to his death. Then, slowly, she approached, and once more Howland held her hands clasped to him and gazed questioningly down into the wild eyes that stared into his own.

"Why did you run away from me?" were the first words that he spoke. They came from him gently, as if he had known her for a long time. In them there was no tone of bitterness; in the warmth of his gray eyes there was none of the denunciation which she might have expected. He repeated the question, bending his head until

he felt the soft touch of her hair on his lips.
"Why did you run away from me?"

She drew away from him, her eyes searching
his face.

"I lied to you," she breathed, her words coming to him in a whisper. "I lied—"

The words caught in her throat. He saw her
struggling to control herself, to stop the quivering of her lip, the tremble in her voice. In another moment she had broken down, and with a
low, sobbing cry sank in a chair beside the
table and buried her head in her arms. As
Howland saw the convulsive trembling of her
shoulders, his soul was flooded with a strange
joy—not at this sight of her grief, but at the
knowledge that she was sorry for what she had
done. Softly he approached. The girl's fur
cap had fallen off. Her long, shining braid
was half undone and its silken strands fell over
her shoulder and glistened in the lamp-glow
on the table. His hand hesitated, and then fell
gently on the bowed head.

"Sometimes the friend who lies is the only friend who's true," he said. "I believe that it was necessary for you to—lie."

Just once his hand stroked her soft hair, then, catching himself, he went to the opposite side of the narrow table and sat down. When the girl raised her head there was a bright flush in her cheeks. He could see the damp stain of tears on her face, but there was no sign of them now in the eyes that seemed seeking in his own the truth of his words, spoken a few moments before.

"You believe that?" she questioned eagerly. "You believe that it was necessary for me to—lie?" She leaned a little toward him, her fingers twining themselves about one another nervously, as she waited for him to answer.

"Yes," said Howland. He spoke the one word with a finality that sent a gladness into the soft brown eyes across from him. "I believe that you *had* to lie to me."

His low voice was vibrant with unbounded

90

faith. Other words were on his lips, but he forced them back. A part of what he might have said—a part of the strange, joyous tumult in his heart—betrayed itself in his face, and before that betrayal the girl drew back slowly, the color fading from her cheeks.

"And I believe you will not lie to me again," he said.

She rose to her feet and flung back her hair, looking down on him in the manner of one who had never before met this kind of man, and knew not what to make of him.

"No, I will not lie to you again," she replied, more firmly. "Do you believe me now?"

"Yes."

"Then go back into the South. I have come to tell you that again to-night—to *make* you believe me. You should have turned back at Le Pas. If you don't go—to-morrow—"

Her voice seemed to choke her, and she stood without finishing, leaving him to understand what she had meant to say. In an instant Howland was at her side. Once more his old, resolute fighting blood was up. Firmly he took her hands again, his eyes compelling her to look up at him.

"If I don't go to-morrow—they will kill me," he completed, repeating the words of her note to him. "Now, if you are going to be honest with me, tell me this—*who* is going to kill me, and *why?*"

He felt a convulsive shudder pass through her as she answered,

"I said that I would not lie to you again. If I can not tell you the truth I will tell you nothing. It is impossible for me to say why your life is in danger."

"But you know?"

"Yes."

He seated her again in the chair beside the table and sat down opposite her.

"Will you tell me who you are?"

She hesitated, twisting her fingers nervously in a silken strand of her hair.

"Will you?" he persisted.

"If I tell you who I am," she said at last, "you will know who is threatening your life."

He stared at her in astonishment.

"The devil, you say!" The words slipped from his lips before he could stop them. For a second time the girl rose from her chair.

"You will go?" she entreated. "You will go to-morrow?"

Her hand was on the latch of the door.

"You will go?"

He had risen, and was lighting a cigar over the chimney of the lamp. Laughing, he came toward her.

"Yes, surely I am going—to see you safely home." Suddenly he turned back to the lounge and belted on his revolver and holster. When he returned she barred his way defiantly, her back against the door.

"You can not go!"

"Why?"

"Because—" He caught the frightened

93

flutter of her voice again. "Because they will kill you!"

The low laugh that he breathed in her hair was more of joy than fear.

"I am glad that you care," he whispered to her softly.

"You must go!" she still persisted.

"With you, yes," he answered.

"No, no—to-morrow. You must go back to Le Pas—back into the South. Will you promise me that?"

"Perhaps," he said. "I will tell you soon." She surrendered to the determination in his voice and allowed him to pass out into the night with her. Swiftly she led him along a path that ran into the deep gloom of the balsam and spruce. He could hear the throbbing of her heart and her quick, excited breathing as she stopped, one of her hands clasping him nervously by the arm.

"It is not very far—from here," she whispered. "You must not go with me. If they saw me with you—at this hour—" He felt her shuddering against him.

"Only a little farther," he begged.

She surrendered again, hesitatingly, and they went on, more slowly than before, until they came to where a few faint lights in the camp were visible ahead of them.

"Now—now you *must* go!"

Howland turned as if to obey. In an instant the girl was at his side.

"You have not promised," she entreated. "Will you go—to-morrow?"

In the luster of the eyes that were turned up to him in the gloom Howland saw again the strange, sweet power that had taken possession of his soul. It did not occur to him in these moments that he had known this girl for only a few hours, that until to-night he had heard no word pass from her lips. He was conscious only that in the space of those few hours something had come into his life which he had never known before; and a deep longing to tell her

95

this, to take her sweet face between his hands, as they stood in the gloom of the forest, and to confess to her that she had become more to him than a passing vision in a strange wilderness filled him. That night he had forgotten half of the strenuous lesson he had striven years to master; success, ambition, the mere joy of achievement, were for the first time sunk under a greater thing for him—the pulsating, human presence of this girl; and as he looked down into her face, pleading with him still in its white, silent terror, he forgot, too, what this woman was or might have been, knowing only that to him she had opened a new and glorious world filled with a promise that stirred his blood like sharp wine. He crushed her hands once more to his breast as he had done on the Great North Trail, holding her so close that he could feel the throbbing of her bosom against him. He spoke no word— and still her eyes pleaded with him to go. Suddenly he freed one of his hands and brushed back the thick hair from her brow and turned her face gently, until what dim light came down from the stars above glowed in the beauty of her eyes. In his own face she saw that which he had not dared to speak, and from her lips there came a soft little sobbing cry.

"No, I have not promised—and I will not promise," he said, holding her face so that she could not look away from him. "Forgive me for—for—doing this—" And before she could move he caught her for a moment close in his arms, holding her so that he felt the quick beating of her heart against his own, the sweep of her hair and breath in his face. "This is why I will not go back," he cried softly. "It is because I love you—love you—"

He caught himself, choking back the words, and as she drew away from him her eyes shone with a glory that made him half reach out his arms to her.

"You will forgive me!" he begged. "I do not mean to do wrong. Only, you must know why I shall not go back into the South."

From her distance she saw his arms stretched like shadows toward her. Her voice was low, so low that he could hardly hear the words she spoke, but its sweetness thrilled him.

"If you love me you will do this thing for me. You will go to-morrow."

"And you?"

"I?" He heard the tremulous quiver in her voice. "Very soon you will forget that you have —ever—seen—me."

From down the path there came the sound of low voices. Excitedly the girl ran to Howland, thrusting him back with her hands.

"Go! Go!" she cried tensely. "Hurry back to the cabin! Lock your door—and don't come out again to-night! Oh, please, if you love me, please, go—"

The voices were approaching. Howland fancied that he could distinguish dark shadows between the thinned walls of the forest. He laughed softly.

"I am not going to run, little girl," he whispered. "See?" He drew his revolver so that it gleamed in the light of the stars.

With a frightened gasp the girl pulled him into the thick bushes beside the path until they stood a dozen paces from where those who were coming down the trail would pass. There was a silence as Howland slipped his weapon back into its holster. Then the voices came again, very near, and at the sound of them his companion shrank close to him, her hands clutching his arms, her white, frightened face raised to him in piteous appeal. His blood leaped through him like fire. He knew that the girl had recognized the voices—that they who were about to pass him were the mysterious enemies against whom she had warned him. Perhaps they were the two who had attacked him on the Great North Trail. His muscles grew tense. The girl could feel them straining under her hands, could feel his body grow rigid and alert. His hand fell again on his revolver; he made a step past her, his eyes flashing, his face as set as iron. Almost sobbing, she pressed herself against his breast, holding him back.

"Don't—don't—don't—" she whispered.

They could hear the cracking of brush under the feet of those who were approaching. Suddenly the sounds ceased not twenty paces away.

From his arms the girl's hands rose slowly to his shoulders, to his face, caressingly, pleadingly; her beautiful eyes glowed, half with terror, half with a prayer to him.

"Don't!" she breathed again, so close that her sweet breath fell warm on his face. "Don't—if you—if you care for me!"

Gently he drew her close in his arms, crushing her face to his breast, kissing her hair, her eyes, her mouth.

"I love you," he whispered again and again.

The steps were resumed, the voices died away. Then there came a pressure against his breast, a gentle resistance, and he opened his arms so that the girl drew back from him. Her lips were smiling at him, and in that smile there was gentle accusation, the sweetness of forgiveness, and he could see that with these there had come also a flush into her cheeks and a dazzling glow into her eyes.

"They are gone," she said tremblingly.

"Yes; they are gone."

He stood looking down into her glowing face in silence. Then, "They are gone," he repeated. "They were the men who tried to kill me at Prince Albert. I have let them go—for you. Will you tell me your name?"

"Yes—that much—now. It is Meleese."

"Meleese!"

The name fell from him sharply. In an instant there recurred to him all that Croisset had said, and there almost came from his lips the half-breed's words, which had burned themselves in his memory, "Perhaps you will understand when I tell you this warning is sent to you by the little Meleese." What had Croisset meant?

"Meleese," he repeated, looking strangely into the girl's face.

"Yes—Meleese—"

She drew back from him slowly, the color fading from her cheeks; and as she saw the light in his eyes, there burst from her a short, stifled cry.

"Now—you understand—you understand why you must go back into the South," she almost sobbed. "Oh, I have sinned to tell you my name! But you will go, won't you? You will go—for me—"

"For you I would go to the end of the earth!" interrupted Howland, his pale face near to her. "But you must tell me why. I don't understand you. I don't know why those men tried to kill me in Prince Albert. I don't know why my life is in danger here. Croisset told me that my warning back there came from a girl named Meleese. I didn't understand him. I don't understand you. It is all a mystery to me. So far as I know I have never had enemies. I never heard your name until Croisset spoke it. What did he mean? What do you mean? Why do you want to drive me from the Wekusko? Why is my life in danger? It is for you to tell me these things. I have been honest with you. I love you. I will fight for you if it is necessary —but you must tell me—tell me—"

His breath was hot in her face, and she stared at him as if what she heard robbed her of the power of speech.

"Won't you tell me?" he whispered, more softly. "Meleese—" She made no effort to resist him as he drew her once more in his arms, crushing her sweet lips to his own. "Meleese, won't you tell me?"

Suddenly she lifted her hands to his face and pushed back his head, looking squarely into his eyes.

"If I tell you," she said softly, "and in telling you I betray those whom I love, will you promise to bring harm to none of them, but g— go back into the South?"

"And leave you?"

"Yes—and leave me."

There was the faintest tremor of a sob in the voice which she was trying so hard to control. His arms tightened about her.

"I will swear to do what is best for you—and for me," he replied. "I will swear to bring harm to none whom you care to shield. But I will not promise to leave you!"

A soft glow came into the girl's eyes as she unclasped his arms and stood back from him.

"I will think—think—" she whispered quickly. "Perhaps I will tell you to-morrow night— here—if you will keep your oath and do what is best for you—and for me."

"I swear it!"

"Then I will meet you here—at this time— when the others are asleep. But—to-morrow— you will be careful—careful—" Unconsciously she half reached her arms out to him as she turned toward the path. "You will be careful— to-morrow—promise me that."

"I promise."

Like a shadow she was gone. He heard her

quick steps running up the path, saw her form as it disappeared in the forest gloom. For a few moments longer he stood, hardly breathing, until he knew that she had gone beyond his hearing. Then he walked swiftly along the footpath that led to the cabin.

CHAPTER VII

THE BLOWING OF THE COYOTE

IN the new excitement that pulsated with every
fiber of his being, Howland forgot his own
danger, forgot his old caution and the fears that
gave birth to it, forgot everything in these moments but Meleese and his own great happiness.
For he was happy, happier than he had ever been
in his life, happier than he had ever expected to
be. He was conscious of no madness in this
strange, new joy that swept through his being
like a fire; he did not stop to weigh with himself
the unreasoning impulses that filled him. He had
held Meleese in his arms, he had told her of his
love, and though she had accepted it with gentle
unresponsiveness he was thrilled by the memory
of that last look in her eyes, which had spoken
faith, confidence, and perhaps even more. And
his faith in her had become as limitless as the blue

space above him. He had known her for but a few hours and yet in that time it seemed to him that he had lived longer than in all of the years that had gone before. She had lied to him, had divulged only a part of her identity—and yet he knew that there were reasons for these things.

To-morrow night he would see her again, and then—

What would she tell him? Whatever it was, it was to be a reward for his own love. He knew that, by the half-fearing tremble of her voice, the sobbing catch of her breath, the soft glow in her eyes. Impelled by that love, would she confide in him? And then—would he go back into the South?

He laughed, softly, joyfully.

Yes, he would go back into the South—he would go to the other end of the earth, if she would go with him. What was the building of this railroad now to that other great thing that had come into his life? For the first time he saw duty in another light. There were others who could build the road; success, fortune, ambition —in the old way he had seen them—were overshadowed now by this love of a girl.

He stopped and lighted his pipe. The fragrant odor of the tobacco, the flavor of the warm smoke in his mouth, helped to readjust him, to cool his heated brain. The old fighting instincts leaped into life again. Go into the South? He asked himself the question once more, and in the gloomy silence of the forest his low laugh fell again as he clenched his hands in anticipation of what was ahead of him. No—he would build the road! And in building it he would win this girl, if it was given for him to possess her.

His saner thoughts brought back his caution. He went more slowly toward the cabin, keeping in the deep shadows and stopping now and then to listen. At the edge of the clearing he paused for a long time. There was no sign of life about the cabin abandoned by Gregson and Thorne. It was probable that the two men who had passed along the path had returned to the camp by another trail, and still keeping as much within the shadows as possible he went to the door and entered.

With his feet propped in front of the big box stove sat Jackpine. The Indian rose as Howland entered, and something in the sullen gloom of his face caused the young engineer to eye him questioningly.

"Any one been here, Jackpine?"

The old sledge-driver gave his head a negative shake and hunched his shoulders, pointing at the same time to the table, on which lay a carefully folded piece of paper.

"Thorne," he grunted.

Howland spread out the paper in the light of the lamp, and read:

"MY DEAR HOWLAND:

"I forgot to tell you that our mail sledge starts for Le Pas to-morrow at noon, and as I'm planning on going down with it I want you to get over as early as you can in the morning. Can put you on to everything in the camp between eight and twelve.   THORNE."

109

A whistle of astonishment escaped Howland's lips.

"Where do you sleep, Jackpine?" he asked suddenly.

"Cabin in edge of woods," replied the Indian.

"How about breakfast? Thorne hasn't put me on to the grub line yet."

"Thorne say you eat with heem in mornin'. I come early—wake you. After heem go—to-morrow—eat here."

"You needn't wake me," said Howland, throwing off his coat. "I'll find Thorne—probably before he's up. Good night."

Jackpine had half opened the door, and for a moment the engineer caught a glimpse of his dark, grinning face looking back over his shoulder. He hesitated, as if about to speak, and then with a mouthful of his inimitable chuckles, he went out.

After bolting the door Howland lighted a small table lamp, entered the sleeping room and prepared for bed.

"Got to have a little sleep no matter if things are going off like a Fourth of July celebration," he grumbled, and rolled between the sheets.

In spite of his old habit of rising with the breaking of dawn it was Jackpine who awakened him a few hours later. The camp was hardly astir when he followed the Indian down among the log cabins to Thorne's quarters. The senior engineer was already dressed.

" ....y to hustle you so, Howland," he greeted, "but I've got to go down with the mail. Just between you and me I don't believe the camp doctor is much on his job. I've got a deuced bad shoulder and a worse arm, and I'm going down to a good surgeon as fast as I can."

"Didn't they send Weston up with you?" asked Howland. He knew that Weston was the best "accident man" in the company's employ.

"Yes—Weston," replied the senior, eying him sharply. "I don't mean to say he's not a good man, Howland," he amended quickly. "But he doesn't quite seem to take hold of this hurt of mine. By the way, I looked over our pay-roll and there is no Croisset on it."

For an hour after breakfast the two men were busy with papers, maps and drawings relative to the camp work. Howland had kept in close touch with operations from Chicago and by the time they were ready to leave for outside inspection he was confident that he could take hold without the personal assistance of either Gregson or Thorne. Before that hour had passed he was certain of at least one other thing—that it was not incompetency that was taking the two senior engineers back to the home office. He had half expected to find the working-end in the same disorganized condition as its chiefs. But if Gregson and Thorne had been laboring under a tremendous strain of some kind it was not reflected in the company's work, as shown in the office records which the latter had spread out before him.

"That's a big six months' work," said Thorne when they had finished. "Good Lord, man, when we first came up here a jack-rabbit couldn't hop through this place where you're sitting, and now see what we've got! Fifty cabins, four mess-halls, two of the biggest warehouses north of Winnipeg, a post-office, a hospital, three blacksmith shops and—a ship-yard!"

"A ship-yard!" exclaimed Howland in genuine surprise.

"Sure, with a fifty-ton ship half built and frozen stiff in the ice. You can finish her in the spring and you'll find her mighty useful for bringing supplies from the head of the Wekusko. We're using horses on the ice now. Had a deuced hard time in getting fifty of 'em up from Le Pas. And besides all this, we've got six miles of road-bed built to the south and three to the north. We've got a sub-camp at each working-end, but most of the men still prefer to come in at night." He dragged himself slowly and painfully to his feet as a knock sounded at the door. "That's MacDonald, our camp superintendent," he explained. "Told him to be here at eight. He's a corker for taking hold of things."

A little, wiry, red-headed man hopped in as Thorne threw open the door. The moment his eyes fell on Howland he sprang forward with outstretched hand, smiling and bobbing his head.

"Howland, of course!" he cried. "Glad to see you! Five minutes late—awful sorry—but they're having the devil's own time over at a coyote we're going to blow this morning, and that's what kept me."

From Howland he whirled on the senior with the sudden movement of a cricket.

"How's the arm, Thorne? And if there's any mercy in your corpus tell me if Jackpine brought me the cigarettes from Le Pas. If he forgot them, as the mail did, I'll have his life as sure—"

"He brought them," said Thorne. "But how about this coyote, Mac? I thought it was ready to fire."

"So it is—now. The south ridge is scheduled to go up at ten o'clock. We'll blow up the big

north mountains sometime to-night. It'll make
a glorious fireworks—one hundred and twenty-
five barrels of powder and four fifty-pound cases
of dynamite—and if you can't walk that far,
Thorne, we'll take you up on a sledge. Mustn't
allow you to miss it!"

"Sorry, but I'll have to, Mac. I'm going
south with the mail. That's why I want you
with Howland and me this morning. It will be
up to you to get him acquainted with every detail in camp."

"Bully!" exclaimed the little superintendent,
rubbing his hands with brisk enthusiasm.
"Greggy and Thorne have done some remark-
able things, Mr. Howland. You'll open your
eyes when you see 'em! Talk about building
railroads! We've got 'em all beat a thousand
ways—tearing through forests, swamps and
those blooming ridge-mountains—and here we
are pretty near up at the end of the earth. The
new Trans-continental isn't in it with us!
The—"

"Ring off, Mac!" exclaimed Thorne; and Howland found himself laughing down into the red, freckled face of the superintendent. He liked this man immensely from the first.

"He's a bunch of live wires, double-charged all the time," said Thorne in a low voice as Mac-Donald went out ahead of them. "Always like that—happy as a boy most of the time, loved by the men, but the very devil himself when he's riled. Don't know what this camp would do without him."

This same thought occurred to Howland a dozen times during the next two hours. Mac-Donald seemed to be the life and law of the camp, and he wondered more and more at Thorne's demeanor. The camp chiefs and gang foremen whom they met seemed to stand in a certain awe of the senior engineer, but it was at the little red-headed Scotchman's cheery words that their eyes lighted with enthusiasm. This was not like the old Thorne, who had been the eye, the ear and the tongue of the company's greatest en

116

gineering works for a decade past, and whose boundless enthusiasm and love of work had been the largest factors in the winning of fame that was more than national. He began to note that there was a strange nervousness about Thorne when they were among the men, an uneasy alertness in his eyes, as though he were looking for some particular face among those they encountered. MacDonald's shrewd eyes observed his perplexity, and once he took an opportunity to whisper:

"I guess it's about time for Thorne to get back into civilization. There's something bad in his system. Weston told me yesterday that his injuries are coming along finely. I don't understand it."

A little later they returned with Thorne to his room.

"I want Howland to see this south coyote go up," said MacDonald. "Can you spare him? We'll be back before noon."

"Certainly. Come and take dinner with me at

117

twelve. That will give me time to make memoranda of things I may have forgotten."

Howland fancied that there was a certain tone of relief in the senior's voice, but he made no mention of it to the superintendent as they walked swiftly to the scene of the "blow-out." The coyote was ready for firing when they arrived. The coyote itself—a tunnel of fifty feet dug into the solid rock of the mountain and terminating in a chamber packed with explosives—was closed by masses of broken rock, rammed tight, and MacDonald showed his companion where the electric wire passed to the fuse within.

"It's a confounded mystery to me why Thorne doesn't care to see this ridge blown up!" he exclaimed after they had finished the inspection. "We've been at work for three months drilling this coyote, and the bigger one to the north. There are four thousand square yards of rock to come out of there, and six thousand out of the other. You don't see shots like those three times in a lifetime, and there'll not be another

118

for us between here and the bay. What's the matter with Thorne?"

Without waiting for a reply MacDonald walked swiftly in the direction of a ridge to the right. Already guards had been thrown out on all sides of the mountain and their thrilling warnings of "Fire—Fire—Fire," shouted through megaphones of birch-bark, echoed with ominous meaning through the still wilderness, where for the time all work had ceased. On the top of the ridge half a hundred of the workmen had already assembled, and as Howland and the superintendent came among them they fell back from around a big, flat boulder on which was stationed the electric battery. MacDonald's face was flushed and his eyes snapped like dragon-flies as he pointed to a tiny button.

"God, but I can't understand why Thorne doesn't care to see this," he said again. "Think of it, man—seven thousand five hundred pounds of powder and two hundred of dynamite! A touch of this button, a flash along the wire, and the fuse is struck. Then, four or five minutes, and up goes a mountain that has stood here since the world began. Isn't it glorious?" He straightened himself and took off his hat. "Mr. Howland, will you press the button?"

With a strange thrill Howland bent over the battery, his eyes turned to the mass of rock looming sullen and black half a mile away, as if bidding defiance in the face of impending fate. Tremblingly his finger pressed on the little white knob, and a silence like that of death fell on those who watched. One minute—two—three—five passed, while in the bowels of the mountain the fuse was sizzling to its end. Then there came a puff, something like a cloud of dust rising skyward, but without sound; and before its upward belching had ceased a tongue of flame spurted out of its crest—and after that, perhaps two seconds later, came the explosion. There was a rumbling and a jarring, as if the earth were convulsed under foot; volumes of dense black smoke shot upward, shutting the mountain in

an impenetrable pall of gloom; and in an instant these rolling, twisting volumes of black became lurid, and an explosion like that of a thousand great guns rent the air. As fast as the eye could follow, sheets of flame shot out of the sea of smoke, climbing higher and higher, in lightning flashes, until the lurid tongues licked the air a quarter of a mile above the startled wilderness. Explosion followed explosion, some of them coming in hollow, reverberating booms, others sounding as if in mid-air. The heavens were filled with hurtling rocks; solid masses of granite ten feet square were thrown a hundred feet away; rocks weighing a ton were hurled still farther, as if they were no more than stones flung by the hand of a giant; chunks that would have crashed from the roof to the basement of a sky-scraper dropped a third and nearly a half a mile away. For three minutes the frightful convulsions continued. Then the lurid lights died out of the pall of smoke, and the pall itself began to settle. Howland felt a grip on his arm. Dumbly he turned and looked into the white, staring face of the superintendent. His ears tingled, every fiber in him seemed unstrung. MacDonald's voice came to him strange and weird.

"What do you think of *that*, Howland?"

The two men gripped hands, and when they looked again they saw dimly through dust and smoke only torn and shattered masses of rock where had been the giant ridge that barred the path of the new road to the bay.

Howland talked but little on their way back to camp. The scene that he had just witnessed affected him strangely; it stirred once more within him all of his old ambition, all of his old enthusiasm, and yet neither found voice in words. He was glad when the dinner was over at Thorne's, and with the going of the mail sledge and the senior engineer there came over him a still deeper sense of joy. Now *he* was in charge; it was *his* road from that hour on. He crushed MacDonald's hand in a grip that meant more than words when they parted. In his own cabin he threw off his coat and hat, lighted his pipe, and tried to realize just what this all meant for him. He was in charge—in charge of the greatest railroad building job on earth—*he*, Jack Howland, who less than twenty years ago was a barefooted, half-starved urchin peddling papers in the streets where he was now famous! And now what was this black thing that had come up to threaten his chances just as he had about won his great fight? He clenched his hands as he thought again of what had already happened— the cowardly attempt on his life, the warnings, and his blood boiled to fever heat. That night —after he had seen Meleese—he would know what to do. But he would not be driven away, as Gregson and Thorne had been driven. He was determined on that.

The gloom of night falls early in the great northern mid-winter, and it was already growing dusk when there came the sound of a voice outside, followed a moment later by a loud knock at the door. At Howland's invitation the door opened and the head and shoulders of a man appeared.

"Something has gone wrong out at the north coyote, sir, and Mr. MacDonald wants you just as fast as you can get out there," he said. "He sent me down for you with a sledge."

"MacDonald told me the thing was ready for firing," said Howland, putting on his hat and coat. "What's the matter?"

"Bad packing, I guess. Heard him swearing about it. He's in a terrible sweat to see you."

Half an hour later the sledge drew up close to the place where Howland had seen a score of men packing bags of powder and dynamite earlier in the day. Half a dozen lanterns were burning among the rocks, but there was no sign of movement or life. The engineer's companion gave a sudden sharp crack of his long whip and in response to it there came a muffled halloo from out of the gloom.

"That's MacDonald, sir. You'll find him

right up there near that second light, where the coyote opens up. He's grilling the life out of half a dozen men in the chamber, where he found the dynamite on top of the powder instead of under it."

"All right!" called back Howland, starting up among the rocks. Hardly had he taken a dozen steps when a dark object shot out behind him and fell with crushing force on his head. With a groaning cry he fell forward on his face. For a few moments he was conscious of voices about him; he knew that he was being lifted in the arms of men, and that after a time they were carrying him so that his feet dragged on the ground. After that he seemed to be sinking down—down—down—until he lost all sense of existence in a chaos of inky blackness.

CHAPTER VIII

THE HOUR OF DEATH

A RED, unwinking eye staring at him fixedly from out of impenetrable gloom—an ogreish, gleaming thing that brought life back into him with a thrill of horror—was Howland's first vision of returning consciousness. It was dead in front of him, on a level with his face—a ball of yellow fire that seemed to burn into his very soul. He tried to cry out, but no sound fell from his lips; he strove to move, to fight himself away, but there was no power of movement in his limbs. The eye grew larger. He saw that it was so bright it cast a halo, and the halo widened before his own staring eyes until the dense gloom about it seemed to be melting away. Then he knew. It was a lantern in front of him, not more than ten feet away. Consciousness flooded him, and he made another effort to cry out,

126

to free his arms from an invisible clutch that held him powerless. At first he thought this was the clutch of human hands; then, as the lantern-light revealed more clearly the things about him and the outlines of his own figure, he saw that it was a rope, and he knew that he was unable to cry out because of something tight and suffocating about his mouth.

The truth came to him swiftly. He had come up to the coyote on a sledge. Some one had struck him. He remembered that men had half-dragged him over the rocks, and these men had bound and gagged him, and left him here, with the lantern staring him in the face. But where was he? He shifted his eyes, straining to penetrate the gloom. Ahead of him, just beyond the light, there was a black wall; he could not move his head, but he saw where that same wall closed in on the left. He turned his gaze upward, and it ended with that same imprisoning barrier of rock. Then he looked down, and the cry of horror that rose in his throat died in a muffled groan. The light fell dimly on a sack—two of them—three—a tightly packed wall of them.

He knew now what had happened. He was imprisoned in the coyote, and the sacks about him were filled with powder. He was sitting on something hard—a box—fifty pounds of dynamite! The cold sweat stood out in beads on his face, glistening in the lantern-glow. From between his feet a thin, white, ghostly line ran out until it lost itself in the blackness under the lantern. It was the fuse, leading to the box of dynamite on which he was sitting!

Madly he struggled at the thongs that bound him until he sank exhausted against the row of powder sacks at his back. Like words of fire the last warning of Meleese burned in his brain—"You must go, to-morrow—to-morrow—or they will kill you!" And this was the way in which he was to die! There flamed before his eyes the terrible spectacle which he had witnessed a few hours before—the holocaust of fire and smoke and thunder that had disrupted a mountain, a chaos of writhing, twisting fury, and in that moment his heart seemed to cease its beating. He closed his eyes and tried to calm himself. Was it possible that there lived men so fiendish as to condemn him to this sort of death? Why had not his enemies killed him out among the rocks? That would have been easier—quicker—less troublesome. Why did they wish to torture him? What terrible thing had he done? Was he mad—mad—and this all a terrible nightmare, a raving and unreal contortion of things in his brain? In this hour of death question after question raced through his head, and he answered no one of them. He sat still for a time, scarcely breathing. There was no sound, save the beating of his own heart. Then there came another, almost unheard at first, faint, thrilling, maddening.

Tick—tick—tick!

It was the beating of his watch. A spasm of horror seized him.

What time was it?

The coyote was to be fired at nine o'clock. It was four when he left his cabin. How long had he been unconscious? Was it time now—now? Was MacDonald's finger already reaching out to that little white button which would send him into eternity?

He struggled again, gnashing furiously at the thing which covered his mouth, tearing the flesh of his wrists as he twisted at the ropes which bound him, choking himself with his efforts to loosen the thong about his neck. Exhausted again, he sank back, panting, half dead. As he lay with closed eyes a little of his reason asserted itself. After all, was he such a coward as to go mad?

Tick—tick—tick!

His watch was beating at a furious rate. Was something wrong with it? Was it going too fast? He tried to count the seconds, but they raced away from him. When he looked again his gaze fell on the little yellow tongue of flame in the lantern globe. It was not the steady, unwinking eye of a few minutes before. There was a sputtering weakness about it now, and as he watched the light grew fainter and fainter. The flame was going out. A few minutes more and he would be in darkness. At first the significance of it did not come to him; then he straightened himself with a jerk that tightened the thong about his neck until it choked him. Hours must have passed since the lantern had been placed on that rock, else the oil would not be burned out of it now!

For the first time Howland realized that it was becoming more and more difficult for him to get breath. The thing about his neck was tightening, slowly, inexorably, like a hot band of steel, and suddenly, because of this tightening, he found that he had recovered his voice.

"This damned rawhide—is pinching—my Adam's apple—"

Whatever had been about his mouth had slipped down and his words sounded hollow and choking in the rock-bound chamber. He tried to raise his voice in a shout, though he knew how futile his loudest shrieks would be. The effort choked him more. His suffering was becoming excruciating. Sharp pains darted like red-hot needles through his limbs, his back tortured him, and his head ached as though a knife had cleft the base of his skull. The strength of his limbs was leaving him. He no longer felt any sensation in his cramped feet. He measured the paralysis creeping up his legs inch by inch, driving the sharp pains before it—and then a groan of horror rose to his lips.

The light had gone out!

As if that dying of the little yellow flame were the signal for his death, there came to his ears a sharp hissing sound, a spark leaped up into the blackness before his eyes, and a slow, creeping glow came toward him over the rock at his feet.

The hour—the minute—the second had come, and MacDonald had pressed the little white button that was to send him into eternity! He did not cry out now. He knew that the end was very near, and in its nearness he found new strength. Once he had seen a man walk to his death on the scaffold, and as the condemned had spoken his last farewell, with the noose about his neck, he had marveled at the clearness of his voice, at the fearlessness of this creature in his last moment on earth.

Now he understood. Inch by inch the fuse burned toward him—a fifth of the distance, a quarter—now a third. At last it reached a half —was almost under his feet. Two minutes more of life. He put his whole strength once again in an attempt to free his hands. This time his attempt was cool, steady, masterful—with death one hundred seconds away. His heart gave a sudden bursting leap into his throat when he felt something give. Another effort—and in the powder-choked vault there rang out a thrilling cry of triumph. His hands were free! He reached forward to the fuse, and this time a moaning, wordless sob fell from him, faint, terrifying, with all the horror that might fill a human soul in its inarticulate note. He could not reach the fuse because of the thong about his neck!

He felt for his knife. He had left it in his room. Sixty seconds more—forty—thirty! He could see the fiery end of the fuse almost at his feet. Suddenly his groping fingers came in contact with the cold steel of his pocket revolver and with a last hope he snatched it forth, stretching down his pistol arm until the muzzle of the weapon was within a dozen inches of the deadly spark. At his first shot the spark leaped, but did not go out. After the second there was no longer the fiery, creeping thing on the floor, and, crushing his head back against the sacks, Howland sat for many minutes as if death had in reality come to him in the moment of his deliverance. After a time, with tedious slowness, he worked a hand into his trousers' pocket, where he carried a pen-knife. It took him a long time to saw through the rawhide thong about his neck. After that he cut the rope that bound his ankles.

He made an effort to rise, but no sooner had he gained his feet than his paralyzed limbs gave way under him and he dropped in a heap on the floor. Very slowly the blood began finding its way through his choked veins again, and with the change there came over him a feeling of infinite restfulness. He stretched himself out, with his face turned to the black wall above, realizing only that he was saved, that he had outwitted his mysterious enemies again, and that he was comfortable. He made no effort to think—to scheme out his further deliverance. He was with the powder and the dynamite, and the powder and the dynamite could not be exploded until human hands came to attach a new fuse. MacDonald would attend to that very soon, so he went off into a doze that was almost sleep. In his half-consciousness there came to him but one sound—that dreadful ticking of his watch. He seemed to have listened to it for hours when there arose another sound—the ticking of another watch.

He sat up, startled, wondering, and then he laughed happily as he heard the sound more distinctly. It was the beating of picks on the rock outside. Already MacDonald's men were at work clearing the mouth of the coyote. In half an hour he would be out in the big, breathing world again.

The thought brought him to his feet. The numbness was gone from his limbs and he could walk about. His first move was to strike a match and look at his watch.

"Half-past ten!"

He spoke the words aloud, thinking of Meleese. In an hour and a half he was to meet her on the trail. Would he be released in time to keep the tryst? How should he explain his imprisonment in the coyote so that he could leave MacDonald without further loss of time? As the sound of the picks came nearer his brain began working faster. If he could only evade explanations until morning—and then reveal the whole dastardly business to MacDonald! There would be time then for those explanations, for the running down of his murderous assailants, and in the while he would be able to keep his appointment with Meleese.

He was not long in finding a way in which this scheme could be worked, and gathering up the severed ropes and rawhide he concealed them between two of the powder sacks so that those who entered the coyote would discover no signs of his terrible imprisonment. Close to the mouth of the tunnel there was a black rent in the wall of rock, made by a bursting charge of dynamite, in which he could conceal himself. When the men were busy examining the broken fuse he would step out and join them. It would look as though he had crawled through the tunnel after them.

Half an hour later a mass of rock rolled down close to his feet, and a few moments after he saw a shadowy human form crawling through the hole it had left. A second followed, and then a third—and the first voice he heard was that of MacDonald.

"Give us the lantern, Bucky," he called back, and a gleam of light shot into the black chamber. The men walked cautiously toward the fuse, and Howland saw the little superintendent fall on his knees.

"What in hell!" he heard him exclaim, and then there was a silence. As quietly as a cat Howland worked himself to the entrance and made a clatter among the rocks. It was he who responded to the voice.

"What's up, MacDonald?"

He coolly joined the little group. MacDonald looked up, and when he saw the new chief bending over him his eyes stared in unbounded wonder.

"Howland!" he gasped.

It was all he said, but in that one word and in the strange excitement in the superintendent's face Howland read that which made him turn quickly to the men, giving them his first command as general-in-chief of the road that was going to the bay.

"Get out of the coyote, boys," he said. "We won't do anything more until morning."

To MacDonald, as the men went out ahead of them, he added in a low voice:

"Guard the entrance to this tunnel with half a dozen of your best men to-night, MacDonald. I know things which will lead me to investigate this to-morrow. I'm going to leave you as soon as I get outside. Spread the report that it was simply a bad fuse. Understand?"

He crawled out ahead of the superintendent, and before MacDonald had emerged from the coyote he had already lost himself in the starlit gloom of the night and was hastening to his tryst with the beautiful girl, who, he believed, would reveal to him at least a part of one of the strangest and most diabolical plots that had ever originated in the brain of man.

CHAPTER IX

THE TRYST

IT still lacked nearly an hour of the appointed time when Howland came to the secluded spot in the trail where he was to meet Meleese. Concealed in the deep shadows of the bushes he seated himself on the end of a fallen spruce and loaded his pipe, taking care to light it with the flare of the match hidden in the hollow of his hands. For the first time since his terrible experience in the coyote he found himself free to think, and more than ever he began to see the necessity of coolness and of judgment in what he was about to do. Gradually, too, he fought himself back into his old faith in Meleese. His blood was tingling at fever heat in his desire for vengeance, for the punishment of the human fiends who had attempted to blow him to atoms, and yet at the same time there was no bitterness

140

in him toward the girl. He was sure that she
was an unwilling factor in the plot, and that she
was doing all in her power to save him. At the
same time he began to realize that he should no
longer be influenced by her pleading. He had
promised—in return for her confidence this night
—to leave unpunished those whom she wished to
shield. He would take back that promise. Before
she revealed anything to him he would warn her
that he was determined to discover those who had
twice sought to kill him.

It was nearly midnight when he looked at his
watch again. Was it possible that Meleese
would not come? He could not bring himself
to believe that she knew of his imprisonment in
the coyote—of this second attempt on his life.
And yet—if she did—

He rose from the log and began pacing
quickly back and forth in the gloom, his
thoughts racing through his brain with increas-
ing apprehension. Those who had imprisoned
him had learned of his escape an hour ago.

141

Many things might have happened in that time. Perhaps they were fleeing from the camp. Frightened by their failure, and fearing the punishment which would be theirs if discovered, it was not improbable that even now they were many miles from the Wekusko, hurrying deeper into the unknown wilderness to the north. And Meleese would be with them!

Suddenly he heard a step, a light, running step, and with a recognizing cry he sprang out into the starlight to meet the slim, panting, white-faced figure that ran to him from between the thick walls of forest trees.

"Meleese!" he exclaimed softly.

He held out his arms and the girl ran straight into them, thrusting her hands against his breast, throwing back her head so that she looked up into his face with great, staring, horror-filled eyes.

"Now—now—" she sobbed, "*now* will you go?"

Her hands left his breast and crept to his

shoulders; slowly they slipped over them, and as Howland pressed her closer, his lips silent, she gave an agonized cry and dropped her head against his shoulder, her whole body torn in a convulsion of grief and terror that startled him.

"You will go?" she sobbed again and again. "You will go—you will go—"

He ran his fingers through her soft hair, crushing his face close to hers.

"No, I am not going, dear," he replied in a low, firm voice. "Not after what happened tonight."

She drew away from him as quickly as if he had struck her, freeing herself even from the touch of his hands.

"I heard—what happened—an hour ago," she said, her voice choking her. "I overheard—them—talking." She struggled hard to control herself. "You must leave the camp—tonight."

In the gloom she saw Howland's teeth gleaming. There was no fear in his smile; he laughed gently down into her eyes as he took her face between his hands again.

"I want to take back the promise that I gave you last night, Meleese. I want to give you a chance to warn any whom you may wish to warn. I shall not return into the South. From this hour begins the hunt for the cowardly devils who have tried to murder me. Before dawn every man on the Wekusko will be in the search, and if we find them there shall be no mercy. Will you help me, or—"

She struck his hands from her face, springing back before he had finished. He saw a sudden change of expression; her lips grew tense and firm; from the death whiteness of her face there faded slowly away the look of soft pleading, the quivering lines of fear. There was a strangeness in her voice when she spoke—something of the hard determination which Howland had put in his own, and yet the tone of it lacked his gentleness and love.

"Will you please tell me the time?"

THE TRYST

The question was almost startling. Howland held the dial of his watch to the light of the stars.

"It is a quarter past midnight."

The faintest shadow of a smile passed over the girl's lips.

"Are you certain that your watch is not fast?" she asked.

In speechless bewilderment Howland stared at her.

"Because it will mean a great deal to you and to me if it is not a quarter past midnight," continued Meleese, a growing glow in her eyes. Suddenly she approached him and put both of her warm hands to his face, holding down his arms with her own. "Listen," she whispered. "Is there nothing—nothing that will make you change your purpose, that will take you back into the South—to-night?"

The nearness of the sweet face, the gentle touch of the girl's hands, the soft breath of her lips, sent a maddening impulse through How-

land to surrender everything to her. For an instant he wavered.

"There might be one—just *one* thing that
would take me away to-night," he replied, his
voice trembling with the great love that thrilled
him. "For you, Meleese, I would give up everything—ambition, fortune, the building of this
road. If I go to-night will you go with me?
Will you promise to be my wife when we reach
Le Pas?"

A look of ineffable tenderness came into the
beautiful eyes so near to his own.

"That is impossible. You will not love me
when you know what I am—what I have done—"

He stopped her.

"Have you done wrong—a great wrong?"

For a moment her eyes faltered; then, hesitatingly, there fell from her lips, "I—don't—
know. I believe I have. But it's not that—it's
not *that!*"

"Do you mean that—that I have no right to
tell you I love you?" he asked. "Do you mean

that it is wrong for you to listen to me? I—I—
took it for granted that you were a—girl—
that—"

"No, no, it is not that," she cried quickly,
catching his meaning. "It is not wrong for
you to love me." Suddenly she asked again,
"Will you please tell me what time it is—now?"

He looked again.

"Twenty-five minutes after midnight."

"Let us go farther up the trail," she whispered. "I am afraid here."

She led the way, passing swiftly beyond the
path that branched out to his cabin. Two hundred yards beyond this a tree had fallen on the
edge of the trail, and seating herself on it Meleese motioned for him to sit down beside her.
Howland's back was to the thick bushes behind
them. He looked at the girl, but she had turned
away her face. Suddenly she sprang from the
log and stood in front of him.

"Now!" she cried. "Now!" and at that signal
Howland's arms were seized from behind, and

147

in another instant he was struggling feebly in the grip of powerful arms which had fastened themselves about him like wire cable, and the cry that rose to his lips was throttled by a hand over his mouth. For an instant he caught a glimpse of the girl's white face as she stood in the trail; then strong hands pulled him back, while others bound his wrists and still others held his legs. Everything had passed in a few seconds. Helplessly bound and gagged he lay on his back in the snow, listening to the low voices that came faintly to him from beyond the bushes. He could understand nothing that they said—and yet he was sure that he recognized among them the voice of Meleese.

The voices became fainter; he heard retreating footsteps, and at last they died away entirely. Through a rift in the trees straight above him the white, cold stars of the night gleamed down on him, and Howland stared up at them fixedly until they seemed to be hopping and dancing about in the skies. He wanted to swear—yell—

fight. In these moments that he lay on his back in the freezing snow a million demons were born in his blood. The girl had betrayed him again! This time he could find no excuse—no pardon for her. She had accepted his love—had allowed him to kiss her, to hold her in his arms—while beneath that hypocrisy she had plotted his downfall a second time. Deliberately she had given the signal for attack, and now—

He heard again the quick, running step that he had recognized on the trail. The bushes behind him parted, and in the white starlight Meleese fell on her knees at his side, her glorious face bending over him in a grief that he had never seen in it before, her eyes shining on him with a great love. Without speaking she lifted his head in the hollow of her arm and crushed her own down against it, kissing him, and softly sobbing his name.

"Good-by," he heard her breathe. "Good-by —good-by—"

He struggled to cry out as she lowered his

149

head back on the snow, to free his hands, to hold her with him—but he saw her face only once more, bending over him; felt the warm pressure of her lips to his forehead, and then again he could hear her footsteps hurrying away through the forest.

CHAPTER X

A RACE INTO THE NORTH

THAT Meleese loved him, that she had taken his head in her arms, and had kissed him, was the one consuming thought in Howland's brain for many minutes after she had left him bound and gagged on the snow. That she had made no effort to free him did not at first strike him as significant. He still felt the sweet, warm touch of her lips, the pressure of her arms, the smothering softness of her hair. It was not until he again heard approaching sounds that he returned once more to a full consciousness of the mysterious thing that had happened. He heard first of all the creaking of a toboggan on the hard crust, then the pattering of dogs' feet, and after that the voices of men. The sounds stopped on the trail a dozen feet away from him.

With a strange thrill he recognized Croisset's voice.

"You must be sure that you make no mistake," he heard the half-breed say. "Go to the water-fall at the head of the lake and heave down a big rock where the ice is open and the water boiling. Track up the snow with a pair of M'seur Howland's high-heeled boots and leave his hat tangled in the bushes. Then tell the superintendent that he stepped on the stone and that it rolled down and toppled him into the chasm. They could never find his body—and they will send down for a new engineer in place of the lost M'seur."

Stupefied with horror, Howland strained his ears to catch the rest of the cold-blooded scheme which he was overhearing, but the voices grew lower and he understood no more that was said until Croisset, coming nearer, called out:

"Help me with the M'seur before you go Jackpine. He is a dead weight with all those rawhides about him."

As coolly as though he were not more than a

chunk of stovewood, Croisset and the Indian came through the bushes, seized him by the head and feet, carried him out into the trail and laid him lengthwise on the sledge.

"I hope you have not caught cold lying in the snow, M'seur," said Croisset, bolstering up the engineer's head and shoulders and covering him with heavy furs. "We should have been back sooner, but it was impossible. Hoo-la, Woonga!" he called softly to his lead-dog. "Get up there, you wolf-hound!"

As the sledge started, with Croisset running close to the leader, Howland heard the low snapping of a whip behind him and another voice urging on other dogs. With an effort that almost dislocated his neck he twisted himself so he could look back of him. A hundred yards away he discerned a second team following in his trail; he saw a shadowy figure running at the head of the dogs, but what there was on the sledge, or what it meant, he could not see or surmise. Mile after mile the two sledges continued without a stop. Croisset did not turn his head; no word fell from his lips, except an occasional signal to the dogs. The trail had turned now straight into the North, and soon Howland could make out no sign of it, but knew only that they were twisting through the most open places in the forests, and that the play of the Polar lights was never over his left shoulder or his right, but always in his face.

They had traveled for several hours when Croisset gave a sudden shrill shout to the rearmost sledge and halted his own. The dogs fell in a panting group on the snow, and while they were resting the half-breed relieved his prisoner of the soft buckskin that had been used as a gag.

"It will be perfectly safe for you to talk now, M'seur, and to shout as loudly as you please," he said. "After I have looked into your pockets I will free your hands so that you can smoke. Are you comfortable?"

"Comfortable—be damned!" were the first words that fell from Howland's lips, and his

154

blood boiled at the sociable way in which Croisset grinned down into his face. "So you're in it, too, eh?—and that lying girl—"

The smile left Croisset's face.

"Do you mean Meleese, M'seur Howland?"

"Yes."

Croisset leaned down with his black eyes gleaming like coals.

"Do you know what I would do if I was her, M'seur?" he said in a low voice, and yet one filled with a threat which stilled the words of passion which the engineer was on the point of uttering. "Do you know what I would do? I would kill you—kill you inch by inch—torture you. That is what I would do."

"For God's sake, Croisset, tell me why,—why—"

Croisset had found Howland's pistol and freed his hands, and the engineer stretched them out entreatingly.

"I would give my life for that girl, Croisset. I told her so back there, and she came to me when

155

I was in the snow and—" He caught himself, adding to what he had left incomplete. "There is a mistake, Croisset. I am not the man they want to kill!"

Croisset was smiling at him again.

"Smoke—and think, M'seur. It is impossible for me to tell you why you should be dead—but you ought to know, unless your memory is shorter than a child's."

He went to the dogs, stirring them up with the cracking of his whip, and when Howland turned to look back he saw a bright flare of light where the other sledge had stopped. A man's voice came from the farther gloom, calling to Croisset in French.

"He tells me I am to take you on alone," said Croisset, after he had replied to the words spoken in a patois which Howland could not understand. "They will join us again very soon."

"They!" exclaimed Howland. "How many will it take to kill me, my dear Croisset?"

A RACE INTO THE NORTH

The half-breed smiled down into his face again.

"You may thank the Blessed Virgin that they are with us," he replied softly. "If you have any hope outside of Heaven, M'seur, it is on that sledge behind."

As he went again to the dogs, straightening the leader in his traces, Howland stared back at the firelit space in the forest gloom. He could see a man adding fuel to the blaze, and beyond him, shrouded in the deep shadows of the trees, an indistinct tangle of dogs and sledge. As he strained his eyes to discover more there was a movement beyond the figure over the fire and the young engineer's heart leaped with a sudden thrill. Croisset's voice sounded in a shrill shout behind him, and at that warning cry in French the second figure sprang back into the gloom. But Howland had recognized it, and the chilled blood in his veins leaped into warm life again at the knowledge that it was Meleese who was trailing behind them on the second sledge!

"When you yell like that give me a little warning if you please, Jean," he said, speaking as coolly as though he had not recognized the figure that had come for an instant into the firelight. "It is enough to startle the life out of one!"

"It is our way of saying good-by, M'seur," replied Croisset with a fierce snap of his whip. "Hoo-la, get along there!" he cried to the dogs, and in half a dozen breaths the fire was lost to view.

Dawn comes at about eight o'clock in the northern mid-winter; beyond the fiftieth degree the first ruddy haze of the sun begins to warm the southeastern skies at nine, and its glow had already risen above the forests before Croisset stopped his team again. For two hours he had not spoken a word to his prisoner and after several unavailing efforts to break the other's taciturnity Howland lapsed into a silence of his own. When he had brought his tired dogs to a halt, Croisset spoke for the first time.

"We are going to camp here for a few hours,"

he explained. "If you will pledge me your word of honor that you will make no attempt to escape I will give you the use of your legs until after breakfast, M'seur. What do you say?"

"Have you a Bible, Croisset?"

"No, M'seur, but I have the cross of our Virgin, given to me by the missioner at York Factory."

"Then I will swear by it—I will swear by all the crosses and all the Bibles in the world that I will make no effort to escape. I am paralyzed, Croisset! I couldn't run for a week!"

Croisset was searching in his pockets.

"*Mon Dieu!*" he cried excitedly, "I have lost it! Ah, come to think, M'seur, I gave the cross to my Mariane before I went into the South. But I will take your word."

"And who is Mariane, Jean? Will she also be in at the 'kill?'"

"Mariane is my wife, M'seur. Ah, *ma belle* Mariane—*ma cheri*—the daughter of an Indian princess and the granddaughter of a *chef de bataillon*, M'seur! Could there be better than that? And she is be-e-e-utiful, M'seur, with hair like the top side of a raven's wing with the sun shining on it, and—"

"You love her a great deal, Jean."

"Next to the Virgin—and—it may be a little better."

Croisset had severed the rope about the engineer's legs, and as he raised his glowing eyes Howland reached out and put both hands on his shoulders.

"And in just that way I love Meleese," he said softly. "Jean, won't you be my friend? I don't want to escape. I'm not a coward. Won't you think of what your Mariane might do, and be a friend to me? You would die for Mariane if it were necessary. And I would die for the girl back on that sledge."

He had staggered to his feet, and pointed into the forests through which they had come.

"I saw her in the firelight, Jean. Why is she following us? Why do they want to kill me? If

160

you would only give me a chance to prove that it
is all a mistake—that I—"

Croisset reached out and took his hand.

"M'seur, I would like to help you," he interrupted. "I liked you that night we came in together from the fight on the trail. I have liked
you since. And yet, if I was in *their* place, I
would kill you even though I like you. It is a
great duty to kill you. They did not do wrong
when they tied you in the coyote. They did not
do wrong when they tried to kill you on the trail.
But I have taken a solemn oath to tell you nothing; nothing beyond this—that so long as you
are with me, and that sledge is behind us, your
life is not in danger. I will tell you nothing
more. Are you hungry, M'seur?"

"Starved!" said Howland.

He stumbled a few steps out into the snow, the
numbness in his limbs forcing him to catch at
trees and saplings to save himself from falling.
He was astonished at Croisset's words and more
confused than ever at the half-breed's assurance

that his life was no longer in immediate peril. To him this meant that Meleese had not only warned him but was now playing an active part in preserving his life, and this conclusion added to his perplexity. Who was this girl who a few hours before had deliberately lured him among his enemies and who was now fighting to save him? The question held a deeper significance for him than when he had asked himself this same thing at Prince Albert, and when Croisset called for him to return to the camp-fire and breakfast he touched once more the forbidden subject.

"Jean, I don't want to hurt your feelings," he said, seating himself on the sledge, "but I've got to get a few things out of my system. I believe this Meleese of yours is a bad woman."

Like a flash Croisset struck at the bait which Howland threw out to him. He leaned a little forward, a hand quivering on his knife, his eyes flashing fire. Involuntarily the engineer recoiled from that animal-like crouch, from the black rage which was growing each instant in the half-breed's face. Yet Croisset spoke softly and without excitement, even while his shoulders and arms were twitching like a forest cat about to spring.

"M'seur, no one in the world must say that about my Mariane, and next to her they must not say it about Meleese. Up there——" and he pointed still farther into the north—"I know of a hundred men between the Athabasca and the bay who would kill you for what you have said. And it is not for Jean Croisset to listen to it here. I will kill you unless you take it back!"

"God!" breathed Howland. He looked straight into Croisset's face. "I'm glad—it's so—Jean," he added slowly. "Don't you understand, man? I love her. I didn't mean what I said. I would kill for her, too, Jean. I said that to find out— what you would do—"

Slowly Croisset relaxed, a faint smile curling his thin lips.

"If it was a joke, M'seur, it was a bad one."

"It wasn't a joke," cried Howland. "It was a

163

serious effort to make you tell me something about Meleese. Listen, Jean—she told me back there that it was not wrong for me to love her, and when I lay bound and gagged in the snow she came to me and—and kissed me. I don't understand——"

Croisset interrupted him.

"Did she do that, M'seur?"

"I swear it."

"Then you are fortunate," smiled Jean softly, "for I will stake my hope in the blessed hereafter that she has never done that to another man, M'seur. But it will never happen again."

"I believe that it will—unless you kill me."

"And I shall not hesitate to kill you if I think that it is likely to happen again. There are others who would kill you—knowing that it has happened but once. But you must stop this talk, M'seur. If you persist I shall put the rawhide over your mouth again."

"And if I object—fight?"

"You have given me your word of honor. Up

164

here in the big snows the keeping of that word is our first law. If you break it I will kill you."

"Good Lord, but you're a cheerful companion," exclaimed Howland, laughing in spite of himself. "Do you know, Croisset, this whole situation has a good deal of humor as well as tragedy about it. I must be a most important cuss, whoever I am. Ask me who I am, Croisset?"

"And who are you, M'seur?"

"I don't know, Jean. Fact, I don't. I used to think that I was a most ambitious young cub in a big engineering establishment down in Chicago. But I guess I was dreaming. Funny dream, wasn't it? Thought I came up here to build a road somewhere through these infernal— no, I mean these beautiful snows—but my mind must have been wandering again. Ever hear of an insane asylum, Croisset? Am I in a big stone building with iron bars at the windows, and are you my keeper, just come in to amuse me for a time? It's kind of you, Croisset, and I hope that some day I shall get my mind back so that I can thank you decently. Perhaps you'll go mad some day, Jean, and dream about pretty girls, and railroads, and forests, and snows—and then I'll be your keeper. Have a cigar? I've got just two left."

"*Mon Dieu!*" gasped Jean. "Yes, I will smoke, M'seur. Is that moose steak good?"

"Fine. I haven't eaten a mouthful since years ago, when I dreamed that I sat on a case of dynamite just about to blow up. Did you ever sit on a case of dynamite just about to blow up, Jean?"

"No, M'seur. It must be unpleasant."

"That dream was what turned my hair white, Jean. See how white it is—whiter than the snow!"

Croisset looked at him a little anxiously as he ate his meat, and at the gathering unrest in his eyes Howland burst into a laugh.

"Don't be frightened, Jean," he spoke soothingly. "I'm harmless. But I promise you that I'll become violent unless something reasonable occurs pretty soon. Hello, are you going to start so soon?"

"Right away, M'seur," said Croisset, who was stirring up the dogs. "Will you walk and run, or ride?"

"Walk and run, with your permission."

"You have it, M'seur, but if you attempt to escape I must shoot you. Run on the right of the dogs—even with me. I will take this side."

Until Croisset stopped again in the middle of the afternoon Howland watched the backward trail for the appearance of the second sledge, but there was no sign of it. Once he ventured to bring up the subject to Croisset, who did no more than reply with a hunch of his shoulders and a quick look which warned the engineer to keep his silence. After their second meal the journey was resumed, and by referring occasionally to his compass Howland observed that the trail was swinging gradually to the eastward. Long before dusk exhaustion compelled him to ride once more on the sledge. Croisset seemed tireless, and under the early glow of the stars and the red moon he still led on the worn pack until at last it stopped on the summit of a mountainous ridge, with a vast plain stretching into the north as far as the eyes could see through the white gloom. The half-breed came back to where Howland was seated on the sledge.

"We are going but a little farther, M'seur," he said. "I must replace the rawhide over your mouth and the thongs about your wrists. I am sorry—but I will leave your legs free."

"Thanks," said Howland. "But, really, it is unnecessary, Croisset. I am properly subdued to the fact that fate is determined to play out this interesting game of ball with me, and no longer knowing where I am, I promise you to do nothing more exciting than smoke my pipe if you will allow me to go along peaceably at your side."

Croisset hesitated.

"You will not attempt to escape—and you will hold your tongue?" he asked.

"Yes."

Jean drew forth his revolver and deliberately cocked it.

"Bear in mind, M'seur, that I will kill you if you break your word. You may go ahead."

And he pointed down the side of the mountain.

CHAPTER XI

HALF-WAY down the ridge a low word from Croisset stopped the engineer. Jean had toggled his team with a stout length of babeesh on the mountain top and he was looking back when Howland turned toward him. The sharp edge of that part of the mountain from which they were descending stood out in a clear-cut line against the sky, and on this edge the six dogs of the team sat squat on their haunches, silent and motionless, like strangely carved gargoyles placed there to guard the limitless plains below. Howland took his pipe from his mouth as he watched the staring interest of Croisset. From the man he looked up again at the dogs. There was something in their sphynx-like attitude, in the moveless reaching of their muzzles out into the wonderful starlit mystery of the still

170

night that filled him with an indefinable sense of awe. Then there came to his ears the sound that had stopped Croisset—a low, moaning whine which seemed to have neither beginning nor end, but which was borne in on his senses as though it were a part of the soft movement of the air he breathed—a note of infinite sadness which held him startled and without movement, as it held Jean Croisset. And just as he thought that the thing had died away, the wailing came again, rising higher and higher, until at last there rose over him a single long howl that chilled the blood to his very marrow. It was like the wolf-howl of that first night he had looked on the wilderness, and yet unlike it; in the first it had been the cry of the savage, of hunger, of the unending desolation of life that had thrilled him. In this it was death. He stood shivering as Croisset came down to him, his thin face shining white in the starlight. There was no other sound save the excited beating of life in their own bodies when Jean spoke.

171

"M'seur, our dogs howl like that only when some one is dead or about to die," he whispered. "It was Woonga who gave the cry. He has lived for eleven years and I have never known him to fail."

There was an uneasy gleam in his eyes.

"I must tie your hands, M'seur."

"But I have given you my word, Jean——"

"Your hands, M'seur. There is already death below us in the plain, or it is to come very soon. I must tie your hands."

Howland thrust his wrists behind him and about them Jean twisted a thong of babeesh.

"I believe I understand," he spoke softly, listening again for the chilling wail from the mountain top. "You are afraid that I will kill you."

"It is a warning, M'seur. You might try. But I should probably kill you. As it is——" he shrugged his shoulders as he led the way down the ridge——"as it is, there is small chance of Jean Croisset answering the call."

"May those saints of yours preserve me, Jean,

but this is all very cheerful!" grunted Howland, half laughing in spite of himself. "Now that I'm tied up again, who the devil is there to die—but me?"

"That is a hard question, M'seur," replied the half-breed with grim seriousness. "Perhaps it is your turn. I half believe that it is."

Scarcely were the words out of his mouth when there came again the moaning howl from the top of the ridge.

"You're getting on my nerves, Jean—you and that accursed dog!"

"Silence, M'seur!"

Out of the grim loneliness at the foot of the mountain there loomed a shadow which at first Howland took to be a huge mass of rock. A few steps farther and he saw that it was a building. Croisset gripped him firmly by the arm.

"Stay here," he commanded. "I will return soon."

For a quarter of an hour Howland waited. Twice in that interval the dog howled above him.

He was glad when Croisset appeared out of the gloom.

"It is as I thought, M'seur. There is death down here. Come with me!"

The shadow of the big building shrouded them as they approached. Howland could make out that it was built of massive logs and that there seemed to be neither door nor window on their side. And yet when Jean hesitated for an instant before a blotch of gloom that was deeper than the others, he knew that they had come to an entrance. Croisset advanced softly, sniffing the air suspiciously with his thin nostrils, and listening, with Howland so close to him that their shoulders touched. From the top of the mountain there came again the mournful death-song of old Woonga, and Jean shivered. Howland stared into the blotch of gloom, and still staring he followed Croisset—entered—and disappeared in it. About them was the stillness and the damp smell of desertion. There was no visible sign of life, no breathing, no movement but their own.

174

and yet Howland could feel the half-breed's hand clutch him nervously by the arm as they went step by step into the black and silent mystery of the place. Soon there came a fumbling of Croisset's hand at a latch and they passed through a second door. Then Jean struck a match.

Half a dozen steps away was a table and on the table a lamp. Croisset lighted it, and with a quiet laugh faced the engineer. They were in a low, dungeon-like chamber, without a window and with but the one door through which they had entered. The table, two chairs, a stove and a bunk built against one of the log walls were all that Howland could see. But it was not the barrenness of what he imagined was to be his new prison that held his eyes in staring inquiry on Croisset. It was the look in his companion's face, the yellow pallor of fear—a horror—that had taken possession of it. The half-breed closed and bolted the door, and then sat down beside the table, his thin face peering up through the sickly lamp-glow at the engineer.

"M'seur, it would be hard for you to guess where you are."

Howland waited.

"If you had lived in this country long, M'seur, you would have heard of *la Maison de Mort Rouge*—the House of the Red Death, as you would call it. That is where we are—in the dungeon room. It is a Hudson Bay post, abandoned almost since I can remember. When I was a child the smallpox plague came this way and killed all the people. Nineteen years ago the red plague came again, and not one lived through it in this *Poste de Mort Rouge*. Since then it has been left to the weasels and the owls. It is shunned by every living soul between the Athabasca and the bay. That is why you are safe here."

"Ye gods!" breathed Howland. "Is there anything more, Croisset? Safe from what, man? Safe from what?"

"From those who wish to kill you, M'seur. You would not go into the South, so *la belle*

Meleese has compelled you to go into the North. *Comprenez-vous?*"

For a moment Howland sat as if stunned.

"Do you understand, M'seur?" persisted Croisset, smiling.

"I—I—think I do," replied Howland tensely. "You mean—Meleese—"

Jean took the words from him.

"I mean that you would have died last night, M'seur, had it not been for Meleese. You escaped from the coyote—but you would not have escaped from the other. That is all I can tell you. But you will be safe here. Those who seek your life will soon believe that you are dead, and then we will let you go back. Is that not a kind fate for one who deserves to be cut into bits and fed to the ravens?"

"You will tell me nothing more, Jean?" the engineer asked.

"Nothing—except that while I would like to kill you I have sympathy for you. That, perhaps, is because I once lived in the South. For six years I was with the company in Montreal, where I went to school."

He rose to his feet, tying the flap of his caribou skin coat about his throat. Then he unbolted and opened the door. Faintly there came to them, as if from a great distance, the wailing grief of Woonga, the dog.

"You said there was death here," whispered Howland, leaning close to his shoulder.

"There is one who has lived here since the last plague," replied Croisset under his breath. "He lost his wife and children and it drove him mad. That is why we came down so quietly. He lived in a little cabin out there on the edge of the clearing, and when I went to it to-night there was a sapling over the house with a flag at the end of it. When the plague comes to us we hang out a red flag as a warning to others. That is one of our laws. The flag is blown to tatters by the winds. He is dead."

Howland shuddered.

"Of the smallpox?"

178

"Yes."

For a few moments they stood in silence. Then Croisset added, "You will remain here, M'seur, until I return."

He went out, closing and barring the door from the other side, and Howland seated himself again in the chair beside the table. Fifteen minutes later the half-breed returned, bearing with him a good-sized pack and a two-gallon jug.

"There is wood back of the stove, M'seur. Here is food and water for a week, and furs for your bed. Now I will cut those thongs about your wrists."

"Do you mean to say you're going to leave me here alone—in this wretched prison?" cried Howland.

"*Mon Dieu*, is it not better than a grave, M'seur? I will be back at the end of a week."

The door was partly open and for the last time there came to Howland's ears the mourning howl of the old dog on the mountain top. Almost threateningly he gripped Croisset's arm.

"Jean—if you don't come back—what will happen?"

He heard the half-breed chuckling.

"You will die, M'seur, pleasantly and taking your own time at it, which is much better than dying over a case of dynamite. But I will come back, M'seur. Good-by!"

Again the door was closed and bolted and the sound of Croisset's footsteps quickly died away beyond the log walls. Many minutes passed before Howland thought of his pipe, or a fire. Then, shiveringly, he went to seek the fuel which Jean had told him was behind the stove. The old bay stove was soon roaring with the fire which he built, and as the soothing fumes of his pipe impregnated the damp air of the room he experienced a sensation of comfort which was in strange contrast to the exciting happenings of the past few days.

At last he was alone, with nothing to do for a week but eat, sleep and smoke. He had plenty of tobacco and an inspection of the pack showed

that Croisset had left him well stocked with food.
Tilted back in a chair, with his feet on the table,
he absorbed the cheerful heat from the stove, sent
up clouds of smoke, and wondered if the half-
breed had already started back into the South.
What would MacDonald say when Jackpine came
in with the report that he had slipped to his death
in the waterfall? Probably his first move would
be to send the most powerful team on the Wekusko in pursuit of Gregson and Thorne. The
departing engineers would be compelled to return, and then—

He laughed aloud and began pacing back and
forth across the rotted floor of his prison as he
pictured the consternation of the two seniors.
And then a flush burned in his face and his eyes
glowed as he thought of Meleese. In spite of
himself she had saved him from his enemies, and
he blessed Croisset for having told him the meaning of this flight into the North. Once again she
had betrayed him, but this time it was to save his
life, and his heart leaped in joyous faith at this

proof of her love for him. He believed that he understood the whole scheme now. Even his enemies would think him dead. They would leave the Wekusko and after a time, when it was safe for him to return, he would be given his freedom.

With the passing of the hours gloomier thoughts shadowed these anticipations. In some mysterious way Meleese was closely associated with those who sought his life, and if they disappeared she would disappear with them. He was convinced of that. And then—could he find her again? Would she go into the South—to civilization—or deeper into the untraveled wildernesses of the North? In answer to his question there flashed through his mind the words of Jean Croisset: "M'seur, I know of a hundred men between Athabasca and the bay who would kill you for what you have said." Yes, she would go into the North. Somewhere in that vast desolation of which Jean had spoken he would find her, even though he spent half of his life in the search!

It was past midnight when he spread out the

furs and undressed for bed. He opened the stove door and from the bunk watched the faint flickerings of the dying firelight on the log walls. As slumber closed his eyes he was conscious of a sound—the faint, hungerful, wailing cry to which he had listened that first night near Prince Albert. It was a wolf, and drowsily he wondered how he could hear the cry through the thick log walls of his prison. The answer came to him the moment he opened his eyes, hours later. A bit of pale sunlight was falling into the room and he saw that it entered through a narrow aperture close up to the ceiling. After he had prepared his breakfast he dragged the table under this aperture and by standing on it was enabled to peer through. A hundred yards away was the black edge of the spruce and balsam forest. Between him and the forest, half smothered in the deep snow, was a cabin, and he shuddered as he saw floating over it the little red signal of death of which Croisset had told him the night before.

With the breaking of this day the hours

seemed of interminable length. For a time he amused himself by searching every corner and crevice of his prison room, but he found nothing of interest beyond what he had already discov-, ered. He examined the door which Croisset had barred on him, and gave up all hope of escape in that direction. He could barely thrust his arm through the aperture that opened out on the plague-stricken cabin. For the first time since the stirring beginning of his adventures at Prince Albert a sickening sense of his own impotency began to weigh on Howland. He was a prisoner—penned up in a desolate room in the heart of a wilderness. And he, Jack Howland, a man who had always taken pride in his physical prowess, had allowed one man to place him there.

His blood began to boil as he thought of it. Now, as he had time and silence in which to look back on what had happened, he was enraged at the pictures that flashed one after another before him. He had allowed himself to be used as nothing more than a pawn in a strange and mysteri-

ous game. It was not through his efforts alone
that he had been saved in the fight on the Saskatchewan trail. Blindly he had walked into the
trap at the coyote. Still more blindly he had
allowed himself to be led into the ambush at the
Wekusko camp. And more like a child than a
man he had submitted himself to Jean Croisset!

He stamped back and forth across the room,
smoking viciously, and his face grew red with
the thoughts that were stirring venom within
him. He placed no weight on circumstances; in
these moments he found no excuse for himself.
In no situation had he displayed the white
feather, at no time had he felt a thrill of fear.
His courage and recklessness had terrified
Meleese, had astonished Croisset. And yet—what
had he done? From the beginning—from the
moment he first placed his foot in the Chinese
café—his enemies had held the whip-hand. He
had been compelled to play a passive part. Up
to the point of the ambush on the Wekusko trail
he might have found some vindication for him-

self. But this experience with Jean Croisset—it was enough to madden him, now that he was alone, to think about it. Why had *he* not taken advantage of Jean, as Jackpine and the Frenchman had taken advantage of him?

He saw now what he might have done. Somewhere, not very far back, the sledge carrying Meleese and Jackpine had turned into the unknown. They two were alone. Why had he not made Croisset a prisoner, instead of allowing himself to be caged up like a weakling? He swore aloud as there dawned on him more and more a realization of the opportunity he had lost. At the point of a gun he could have forced Croisset to overtake the other sledge. He could have surprised Jackpine, as they had surprised him on the trail. And then? He smiled, but there was no humor in the smile. He at least would have held the whip-hand. And what would Meleese have done?

He asked himself question after question, answering them quickly and decisively in the same breath. Meleese loved him. He would have staked his life on that. His blood leaped as he felt again the thrill of her kisses when she had come to him as he lay bound and gagged beside the trail. She had taken his head in her arms, and through the grief of her face he had seen shining the light of a great love that had glorified it for all time for him. She loved him! And he had let her slip away from him, had weakly surrendered himself at a moment when everything that he had dreamed of might have been within his grasp. With Jackpine and Croisset in his power—

He went no further. Was it too late to do these things now? Croisset would return. With a sort of satisfaction it occurred to him that his actions had disarmed the Frenchman of suspicion. He believed that it would be easy to overcome Croisset, to force him to follow in the trail of Meleese and Jackpine. And that trail? It would probably lead to the very stronghold of his enemies. But what of that? He loaded his

187

pipe again, puffing out clouds of smoke until the room was thick with it. That trail would take him to Meleese—wherever she was. Heretofore his enemies had come to him; now he would go to them. With Croisset in his power, and with none of his enemies aware of his presence, everything would be in his favor. He laughed aloud as a sudden thrilling thought flashed into his mind. As a last resort he would use Jean as a decoy.

He foresaw how easy it would be to bring Meleese to him—to see Croisset. His own presence would be like the dropping of a bomb at her feet. In that moment, when she saw what he was risking for her, that he was determined to possess her, would she not surrender to the pleading of his love? If not he would do the other thing— that which had brought the joyous laugh to his lips. All was fair in war and love, and theirs was a game of love. Because of her love for him Meleese had kidnapped him from his post of duty, had sent him a prisoner to this death-house in the wilderness. Love had exculpated her. That

same love would exculpate him. He would make
her a prisoner, and Jean should drive them back
to the Wekusko. Meleese herself had set the
pace and he would follow it. And what woman,
if she loved a man, would not surrender after
this? In their sledge trip he would have her to
himself, for not only an hour or two, but for
days. Surely in that time he could win. There
would be pursuit, perhaps; he might have to
fight—but he was willing, and a trifle anxious,
to fight.

He went to bed that night, and dreamed of
things that were to happen. A second day, a
third night, and a third day came. With each
hour grew his anxiety for Jean's return. At
times he was almost feverish to have the affair
over with. He was confident of the outcome, and
yet he did not fail to take the Frenchman's true
measurement. He knew that Jean was like live
wire and steel, as agile as a cat, more than a
match with himself in open fight despite his own
superior weight and size. He devised a dozen

189

schemes for Jean's undoing. One was to leap on him while he was eating; another to spring on him and choke him into partial insensibility as he knelt beside his pack or fed the fire; a third to strike a blow from behind that would render him powerless. But there was something in this last that was repugnant to him. He remembered that Jean had saved his life, that in no instance had he given him physical pain. He would watch for an opportunity, take advantage of the Frenchman, as Croisset had taken advantage of him, but he would not hurt him seriously. It should be as fair a struggle as Jean had offered him, and with the handicap in his favor the best man would win.

On the morning of the fourth day Howland was awakened by a sound that came through the aperture in the wall. It was the sharp yelping bark of a dog, followed an instant later by the sharper crack of a whip, and a familiar voice.

Jean Croisset had returned!

With a single leap he was out of his bunk.

Half dressed he darted to the door, and crouched there, the muscles of his arms tightening, his body tense with the gathering forces within him.

The spur of the moment had driven him to quick decision. His opportunity would come when Jean Croisset passed through that door!

CHAPTER XII

THE FIGHT

BEYOND the door Howland heard Jean pause. There followed a few moments silence, as though the other were listening for sound within. Then there came a fumbling at the bar and the door swung inward.

"*Bon jour*, M'seur," called Jean's cheerful voice as he stepped inside. "Is it possible you are not up, with all this dog-barking and—"

His eyes had gone to the empty bunk. Despite his cheerful greeting Howland saw that the Frenchman's face was haggard and pale as he turned quickly toward him. He observed no further than that, but flung his whole weight on the unprepared Croisset, and together they crashed to the floor. There was scarce a struggle and Jean lay still. He was flat on his back, his arms pinioned to his sides, and bringing himself astride the Frenchman's body so that each knee imprisoned an arm Howland coolly began looping the babeesh thongs that he had snatched from the table as he sprang to the door. Behind Howland's back Jean's legs shot suddenly upward. In a quick choking clutch of steel-like muscle they gripped about his neck like powerful arms and in another instant he was twisted backward with a force that sent him half neck-broken to the opposite wall. He staggered to his feet, dazed for a moment, and Jean Croisset stood in the middle of the floor, his caribou skin coat thrown off, his hands clenched, his eyes darkening with a dangerous fire. As quickly as it had come, the fire died away, and as he advanced slowly, his shoulders hunched over, his white teeth gleamed in a smile. Howland smiled back, and advanced to meet him. There was no humor, no friendliness in the smiles. Both had seen that flash of teeth and deadly scintillation of eyes at other times, both knew what it meant.

"I believe that I will kill you, M'seur," said

Jean softly. There was no excitement, no tremble of passion in his voice. "I have been thinking that I ought to kill you. I had almost made up my mind to kill you when I came back to this *Maison de Mort Rouge*. It is the justice of God that I kill you!"

The two men circled, like beasts in a pit, Howland in the attitude of a boxer, Jean with his shoulders bent, his arms slightly curved at his side, the toes of his moccasined feet bearing his weight. Suddenly he launched himself at the other's throat.

In a flash Howland stepped a little to one side and shot out a crashing blow that caught Jean on the side of the head and sent him flat on his back. Half-stunned Croisset came to his feet. It was the first time that he had ever come into contact with science. He was puzzled. His head rang, and for a few moments he was dizzy. He darted in again, in his old, quick, cat-like way, and received a blow that dazed him. This time he kept his feet.

THE FIGHT

"I am sure now that I am going to kill you, M'seur," he said, as coolly as before.

There was something terribly calm and decisive in his voice. He was not excited. He was not afraid. His fingers did not go near the weapons in his belt, and slowly the smile faded from Howland's lips as Jean circled about him. He had never fought a man of this kind; never had he looked on the appalling confidence that was in his antagonist's eyes. From those eyes, rather than from the man, he found himself slowly retreating. They followed him, never taking themselves from his face. In them the fire returned and grew deeper. Two dull red spots began to glow in Croisset's cheeks, and he laughed softly when he suddenly leaped in so that Howland struck at him—and missed. He knew what to expect now. And Howland knew what to expect.

It was the science of one world pitted against that of another—the science of civilization against that of the wilderness. Howland was

trained in his art. For sport Jean had played
with wounded lynx; his was the quickness of
sight, of instinct—the quickness of the great
north loon that had often played this same game
with his rifle-fire, of the sledge-dog whose rip-
ping fangs carried death so quickly that eyes
could not follow. A third and a fourth time he
came within distance and Howland struck and
missed.

"I am going to kill you," he said again.

To this point Howland had remained cool.
Self-possession in his science he knew to be half
the battle. But he felt in him now a slow, swell-
ing anger. The smiling flash in Jean's eyes
began to irritate him; the fearless, taunting
gleam of his teeth, his audacious confidence, put
him on edge. Twice again he struck out swiftly,
but Jean had come and gone like a dart. His
lithe body, fifty pounds lighter than Howland's,
seemed to be that of a boy dodging him in some
tantalizing sport. The Frenchman made no effort at attack; his were the tactics of the wolf

196

at the heels of the bull moose, of the lynx before the prongs of a cornered buck—tiring, worrying, ceaseless.

Howland's striking muscles began to ache and his breath was growing shorter with the exertions which seemed to have no effect on Croisset. For a few moments he took the aggressive, rushing Jean to the stove, behind the table, twice around the room—striving vainly to drive him into a corner, to reach him with one of the sweeping blows which Croisset evaded with the lightning quickness of a hell-diver. When he stopped, his breath came in wind-broken gasps. Jean drew nearer, smiling, ferociously cool.

"I am going to kill you, M'seur," he repeated again.

Howland dropped his arms, his fingers relaxed, and he forced his breath between his lips as if he were on the point of exhaustion. There were still a few tricks in his science, and these, he knew, were about his last cards. He backed into a corner, and Jean followed, his eyes flashing a steely light, his body growing more and more tense.

"Now, M'seur, I am going to kill you," he said in the same low voice. "I am going to break your neck."

Howland backed against the wall, partly turned as if fearing the other's attack, and yet without strength to repel it. There was a contemptuous smile on Croisset's lips as he poised himself for an instant. Then he leaped in, and as his fingers gripped at the other's throat Howland's right arm shot upward in a deadly short-arm punch that caught his antagonist under the jaw. Without a sound Jean staggered back, tottered for a moment on his feet, and fell to the floor. Fifty seconds later he opened his eyes to find his hands bound behind his back and Howland standing at his feet.

"*Mon Dieu*, but that was a good one!" he gasped, after he had taken a long breath or two. "Will you teach it to me, M'seur?"

"Get up!" commanded Howland. "I have no

198

time to waste, Croisset." He caught the French-man by the shoulders and helped him to a chair near the table. Then he took possession of the other's weapons, including the revolver which Jean had taken from him, and began to dress. He spoke no word until he was done.

"Do you understand what is going to happen, Croisset?" he cried then, his eyes blazing hotly. "Do you understand that what you have done will put you behind prison bars for ten years or more? Does it dawn on you that I'm going to take you back to the authorities, and that as soon as we reach the Wekusko I'll have twenty men back on the trail of these friends of yours?"

A gray pallor spread itself over Jean's thin face.

"The great God, M'seur, you can not do that!"

"*Can not!*" Howland's fingers dug into the edge of the table. "By this great God of yours, Croisset, but I will! And why not? Is it because Meleese is among this gang of cut-throats and

199

murderers? Pish, my dear Jean, you must be a fool. They tried to kill me on the trail, tried it again in the coyote, and you came back here determined to kill me. You've held the whip-hand from the first. Now it's mine. I swear that if I take you back to the Wekusko we'll get you all."

"*If*, M'seur?"

"Yes—*if*."

"And that 'if'—" Jean was straining against the table.

"It rests with you, Croisset. I will bargain with you. Either I shall take you back to the Wekusko, hand you over to the authorities and send a force after the others—or you shall take me to Meleese. Which shall it be?"

"And if I take you to Meleese, M'seur?"

Howland straightened, his voice trembling a little with excitement.

"If you take me to Meleese, and swear to do as I say, I shall bring no harm to you or your friends."

THE FIGHT

"And Meleese—" Jean's eyes darkened again. "You will not harm her, M'seur?"

"Harm *her!*" There was a laughing tremor in Howland's voice. "Good God, man, are you so blind that you can't see that I am doing this because of her? I tell you that I love her, and that I am willing to die in fighting for her. Until now I haven't had the chance. You and your friends have played a cowardly underhand game, Croisset. You have taken me from behind at every move, and now it's up to you to square yourself a little or there's going to be hell to pay. Understand? You take me to Meleese or there'll be a clean-up that will put you and the whole bunch out of business. *Harm her—*" Again Howland laughed, leaning his white face toward Jean. "Come, which shall it be, Croisset?"

A cold glitter, like the snap of sparks from striking steels, shot from the Frenchman's eyes. The grayish pallor went from his face. His teeth gleamed in the enigmatic smile that had half undone Howland in the fight.

201

"You are mistaken in some things, M'seur," he said quietly. "Until to-day I have fought for you and not against you. But now you have left me but one choice. I will take you to Meleese, and that means—"

"Good!" cried Howland.

"La, la, M'seur—not so good as you think. It means that as surely as the dogs carry us there you will never come back. *Mon Dieu*, your death is certain!"

Howland turned briskly to the stove.

"Hungry, Jean?" he asked more companionably. "Let's not quarrel, man. You've had your fun, and now I'm going to have mine. Have you had breakfast?"

"I was anticipating that pleasure with you, M'seur," replied Jean with grim humor.

"And then—after I had fed you—you were going to kill me, my dear Jean," laughed Howland, flopping a huge caribou steak on the naked top of the sheet-iron stove. "Real nice fellow you are, eh?"

202

THE FIGHT

"You ought to be killed, M'seur."

"So you've said before. When I see Meleese I'm going to know the reason why, or—"

"Or what, M'seur?"

"Kill you, Jean. I've just about made up my mind that you ought to be killed. If any one dies up where we're going, Croisset, it will be you first of all."

Jean remained silent. A few minutes later Howland brought the caribou steak, a dish of flour cakes and a big pot of coffee to the table. Then he went behind Jean and untied his hands. When he sat down at his own side of the table he cocked his revolver and placed it beside his tin plate. Jean grimaced and shrugged his shoulders.

"It means business," said his captor warningly. "If at any time I think you deserve it I shall shoot you in your tracks, Croisset, so don't arouse my suspicions."

"I took your word of honor," said Jean sarcastically.

"And I will take yours to an extent," replied Howland, pouring the coffee. Suddenly he picked up the revolver. "You never saw me shoot, did you? See that cup over there?" He pointed to a small tin pack-cup hanging to a nail on the wall a dozen paces from them. Three times without missing he drove bullets through it, and smiled across at Croisset.

"I am going to give you the use of your arms and legs, except at night," he said.

"*Mon Dieu*, it is safe," grunted Jean. "I give you my word that I will be good, M'seur."

The sun was up when Croisset led the way outside. His dogs and sledge were a hundred yards from the building, and Howland's first move was to take possession of the Frenchman's rifle and eject the cartridges while Jean tossed chunks of caribou flesh to the huskies. When they were ready to start Jean turned slowly and half reached out a mittened hand to the engineer.

"M'seur," he said softly, "I can not help liking you, though I know that I should have killed you long ago. I tell you again that if you go into the North there is only one chance in a hundred that you will come back alive. Great God, M'seur, up where you wish to go the very trees will fall on you and the carrion ravens pick out your eyes! And that chance—that one chance in a hundred, M'seur—"

"I will take," interrupted Howland decisively.

"I was going to say, M'seur," finished Jean quietly, "that unless accident has befallen those who left Wekusko yesterday that one chance is gone. If you go South you are safe. If you go into the North you are no better than a dead man."

"There will at least be a little fun at the finish," laughed the young engineer. "Come, Jean, hit up the dogs!"

"*Mon Dieu*, I say you are a fool—and a brave man," said Croisset, and his whip twisted sinuously in mid-air and cracked in sharp command over the yellow backs of the huskies.

CHAPTER XIII

THE PURSUIT

BEHIND the sledge ran Howland, to the right of the team ran Jean. Once or twice when Croisset glanced back his eyes met those of the engineer. He cracked his whip and smiled, and Howland's teeth gleamed back coldly in reply. A mutual understanding flashed between them in these glances. In a sudden spurt Howland knew that the Frenchman could quickly put distance between them—but not a distance that his bullets could not cover in the space of a breath. He had made up his mind to fire, deliberately and with his greatest skill, if Croisset made the slightest movement toward escape. If he was compelled to kill or wound his companion he could still go on alone with the dogs, for the trail of Meleese and Jackpine would be as plain as their own, which they were following back into the South.

For the second time since coming into the North he felt the blood leaping through his veins as on that first night in Prince Albert when from the mountain he had heard the lone wolf, and when later he had seen the beautiful face through the hotel window. Howland was one of the few men who possess unbounded confidence in themselves, who place a certain pride in their physical as well as their mental capabilities, and he was confident now. His successful and indomitable fight over obstacles in a big city had made this confidence a genuine part of his being. It was a confidence that flushed his face with joyous enthusiasm as he ran after the dogs, and that astonished and puzzled Jean Croisset.

"*Mon Dieu*, but you are a strange man!" exclaimed the Frenchman when he brought the dogs down to a walk after a half mile run. "Blessed saints, M'seur, you are laughing—and I swear it is no laughing matter."

207

"Shouldn't a man be happy when he is going to his wedding, Jean?" puffed Howland, gasping to get back the breath he had lost.

"But not when he's going to his funeral, M'seur."

"If I were one of your blessed saints I'd hit you over the head with a thunderbolt, Croisset. Good Lord, what sort of a heart have you got inside of your jacket, man? Up there where we're going is the sweetest little girl in the whole world. I love her. She loves me. Why shouldn't I be happy, now that I know I'm going to see her again very soon—and take her back into the South with me?"

"The devil!" grunted Jean.

"Perhaps you're jealous, Croisset," suggested Howland. "Great Scott, I hadn't thought of that!"

"I've got one of my own to love, M'seur; and I wouldn't trade her for all else in the world."

"Damned if I can understand you," swore the engineer. "You appear to be half human; you say you're in love, and yet you'd rather risk your life than help out Meleese and me. What the deuce does it mean?"

"That's what I'm doing, M'seur—helping Meleese. I would have done her a greater service if I had killed you back there on the trail and stripped your body for those things that would be foul enough to eat it. I have told you a dozen times that it is God's justice that you die. And you are going to die—very soon, M'seur."

"No, I'm not going to die, Jean. I'm going to see Meleese, and she's going back into the South with me. And if you're real good you may have the pleasure of driving us back to the Wekusko, Croisset, and you can be my best man at the wedding. What do you say to that?"

"That you are mad—or a fool," retorted Jean, cracking his whip viciously.

The dogs swung sharply from the trail, heading from their southerly course into the northwest.

"We will save a day by doing this," explained

Croisset at the other's sharp word of inquiry. "We will hit the other trail twenty miles west of here, while by following back to where they turned we would travel sixty miles to reach the same point. That one chance in a hundred which you have depends on this, M'seur. If the other sledge has passed——"

He shrugged his shoulders and started the dogs into a trot.

"Look here," cried Howland, running beside him. "Who is with this other sledge?"

"Those who tried to kill you on the trail and at the coyote, M'seur," he answered quickly.

Howland fell half a dozen paces behind. By the end of the first hour he was compelled to rest frequently by taking to the sledge, and their progress was much slower. Jean no longer made answer to his occasional questions. Doggedly he swung on ahead to the right and a little behind the team leader, and Howland could see that for some reason Croisset was as anxious as himself to make the best time possible. His own impatience increased as the morning lengthened. Jean's assurance that the mysterious enemies who had twice attempted his life were only a short distance behind them, or a short distance ahead, set a new and desperate idea at work in his brain. He was confident that these men from the Wekusko were his chief menace, and that with them once out of the way, and with the Frenchman in his power, the fight which he was carrying into the enemy's country would be half won. There would then be no one to recognize him but Meleese.

His heart leaped with joyous hope, and he leaned forward on the sledge to examine Crois-set's empty gun. It was an automatic, and Crois-set, glancing back over the loping backs of the huskies, caught him smiling. He ran more frequently now, and longer distances, and with the passing of each mile his determination to strike a decisive blow increased. If they reached the trail of Meleese and Jackpine before the crossing of the second sledge he would lay in wait for his old enemies; if they had preceded them he would pursue and surprise them in camp. In either case he would possess an overwhelming advantage.

With the same calculating attention to detail that he would have shown in the arrangement of plans for the building of a tunnel or a bridge, he drew a mental map of his scheme and its possibilities. There would be at least two men with the sledge, and possibly three. If they surrendered at the point of his rifle without a fight he would compel Jean to tie them up with dog-traces while he held them under cover. If they made a move to offer resistance he would shoot. With the automatic he could kill or wound the three before they could reach their rifles, which would undoubtedly be on the sledge. The situation had now reached a point where he no longer took into consideration what these men might be to Meleese.

As they continued into the northwest Howland noted that the thicker forest was gradually clearing into wide areas of small banskian pine, and that the rock ridges and dense swamps which had impeded their progress were becoming less numerous. An hour before noon, after a tedious climb to the top of a frozen ridge, Croisset pointed down into a vast level plain lying between them and other great ridges far to the north.

"That is a bit of the Barren Lands that creeps down between those mountains off there, M'seur," he said. "Do you see that black forest that looks like a charred log in the snow to the south and west of the mountains? That is the break that leads into the country of the Athabasca. Somewhere between this point and that we will strike the trail. *Mon Dieu*, I had half expected to see them out there on the plain."

"Who? Meleese and Jackpine, or—"

"No, the others, M'seur. Shall we have dinner here?"

"Not until we hit the trail," replied Howland. "I'm anxious to know about that one chance in a hundred you've given me hope of, Croisset. If they have passed—"

"If they are ahead of us you might just as

well stand out there and let me put a bullet through you, M'seur."

He went to the head of the dogs, guiding them down the rough side of the ridge, while Howland steadied the toboggan from behind. For three-quarters of an hour they traversed the low bush of the plain· in silence. From every rising snow hummock Jean scanned the white desolation about them, and each time, as nothing that was human came within his vision, he turned toward the engineer with a sinister shrug of his shoulders. Once three moving caribou, a mile or more away, brought a quick cry to his lips and Howland noticed that a sudden flush of excitement came into his face, replaced in the next instant by a look of disappointment. After this he maintained a more careful guard over the Frenchman. They had covered less than half of the distance to the caribou trail when in a small open space free of bush Croisset's voice rose sharply and the team stopped.

"What do you think of it, M'seur?" he cried,

pointing to the snow. "What do you think of that?"

Barely cutting into the edge of the open was the broken crust of two sledge trails. For a moment Howland forgot his caution and bent over to examine the trails, with his back to his companion. When he looked up there was a curious laughing gleam in Jean's eyes.

"*Mon Dieu*, but you are careless!" he exclaimed. "Be more careful, M'seur. I may give myself up to another temptation like that."

"The deuce you say!" cried Howland, springing back quickly. "I'm much obliged, Jean. If it wasn't for the moral effect of the thing I'd shake hands with you on that. How far ahead of us do you suppose they are?"

Croisset had fallen on his knees in the trail.

"The crust is freshly broken," he said after a moment. "They have been gone not less than two or three hours, perhaps since morning. See this white glistening surface over the first trail, M'seur, like a billion needle-points growing out

215

of it? That is the work of three or four days' cold. The first sledge passed that long ago."

Howland turned and picked up Croisset's rifle. The Frenchman watched him as he slipped a clip full of cartridges into the breech.

"If there's a snack of cold stuff in the pack dig it out," he commanded. "We'll eat on the run, if you've got anything to eat. If you haven't, we'll go hungry. We're going to over-take that sledge sometime this afternoon or to-night—or bust!"

"The saints be blessed, then we are most cer-tain to bust, M'seur," gasped Jean. "And if we don't the dogs will. *Non*, it is impossible!"

"Is there anything to eat?"

"A morsel of cold meat—that is all. But I say that it is impossible. That sledge—"

Howland interrupted him with an impatient gesture.

"And I say that if there is anything to eat in there, get it out, and be quick about it, Croisset. We're going to overtake those precious friends of yours, and I warn you that if you make any attempt to lose time something unpleasant is going to happen. Understand?"

Jean had bent to unstrap one end of the sledge pack and an angry flash leaped into his eyes at the threatening tone of the engineer's voice. For a moment he seemed on the point of speech, but caught himself and in silence divided the small chunk of meat which he drew from the pack, giving the larger share to Howland as he went to the head of the dogs. Only once or twice during the next hour did he look back, and after each of these glances he redoubled his efforts at urging on the huskies. Before they had come to the edge of the black banskian forest which Jean had pointed out from the farther side of the plain, Howland saw that the pace was telling on the team. The leader was trailing lame, and now and then the whole pack would settle back in their traces, to be urged on again by the fierce cracking of Croisset's long whip. To add to his own discomfiture Howland found that he could no longer keep up with Jean and the dogs, and with this weight added to the sledge the huskies settled down into a tugging walk.

Thus they came into the deep low forest, and Jean, apparently oblivious of the exhaustion of both man and dogs, walked now in advance of the team, his eyes constantly on the thin trail ahead. Howland could not fail to see that his unnecessary threat of a few hours before still rankled in the Frenchman's mind, and several times he made an effort to break the other's taciturnity. But Jean strode on in moody silence, answering only those things which were put to him directly, and speaking not an unnecessary word. At last the engineer jumped from the sledge and overtook his companion.

"Hold on, Jean," he cried. "I've got enough. You're right, and I want to apologize. We're busted—that is, the dogs and I are busted, and we might as well give it up until we've had a feed. What do you say?"

"I say that you have stopped just in time,

M'seur," replied Croisset with purring softness. "Another half hour and we would have been through the forest, and just beyond that—in the edge of the plain—are those whom you seek, Meleese and her people. That is what I started to tell you back there when you shut me up. *Mon Dieu*, if it were not for Meleese I would let you go on. And then—what would happen then, M'seur, if you made your visit to them in broad day? Listen!"

Jean lifted a warning hand. Faintly there came to them through the forest the distant baying of a hound.

"That is one of our dogs from the Mackenzie country," he went on softly, an insinuating triumph in his low voice. "Now, M'seur, that I have brought you here what are you going to do? Shall we go on and take dinner with those who are going to kill you, or will you wait a few hours? Eh, which shall it be?"

For a moment Howland stood motionless, stunned by the Frenchman's words. Quickly he recovered himself. His eyes burned with a metallic gleam as they met the half taunt in Croisset's cool smile.

"If I had not stopped you—we would have gone on?" he questioned tensely.

"To be sure, M'seur," retorted Croisset, still smiling. "You warned me to lose no time—that something would happen if I did."

With a quick movement Howland drew his revolver and leveled it at the Frenchman's heart.

"If you ever prayed to those blessed saints of yours, do it now, Jean Croisset. I'm going to kill you!" he cried fiercely.

CHAPTER XIV

THE GLEAM OF THE LIGHT

IN a single breath the face of Jean Croisset became no more than a mask of what it had been. The taunting smile left his lips and a gray pallor spread over his face as he saw Howland's finger crooked firmly on the trigger of his revolver. In another instant there came the sound of a metallic snap.

"Damnation! An empty cartridge!" Howland exclaimed. "I forgot to load after those three shots at the cup. It's coming this time, Jean!"

Purposely he snapped the second empty cartridge.

"The great God!" gasped Jean. "M'seur—"

From deep in the forest came again the baying of the Mackenzie hound. This time it was much nearer, and for a moment Howland's eyes left the Frenchman's terrified face as he turned his head to listen.

"They are coming!" exclaimed Croisset. "M'seur, I swear to —"

Again Howland's pistol covered his heart.

"Then it is even more necessary that I kill you," he said with frightful calmness. "I warned you that I would kill you if you led me into a trap, Croisset. The dogs are bushed. There is no way out of this but to fight—if there are people coming down the trail. Listen to that!"

This time, from still nearer, came the shout of a man, and then of another, followed by the huskies' sharp yelping as they started afresh on the trail. The flush of excitement that had come into Howland's face paled until he stood as white as the Frenchman. But it was not the whiteness of fear. His eyes were like blue steel flashing in the sunlight.

"There is nothing to do but fight," he repeated, even more calmly than before. "If we were a

mile or two back there it could all happen as I
planned it. But here——"

"They will hear the shots," cried Jean. "The
post is no more than a gunshot beyond the forest,
and there are plenty there who would come out
to see what it means. Quick, M'seur—follow me!
Possibly they are hunters going out to the trap-
lines. If it comes to the worst——"

"What then?" demanded Howland.

"You can shoot me a little later," temporized
the Frenchman with a show of his old coolness.
"*Mon Dieu*, I am afraid of that gun, M'seur.
I will get you out of this if I can. Will you give
me the chance—or will you shoot?"

"I will shoot—if you fail," replied the engineer.

Barely were the words out of his mouth when
Croisset sprang to the head of the dogs, seized
the leader by his neck-trace and half dragged the
team and sledge through the thick bush that
edged the trail. A dozen paces farther on the
dense scrub opened into the clearer run of the

low-hanging banskian through which Jean started at a slow trot, with Howland a yard behind
him, and the huskies following with human-like
cleverness in the sinuous twistings of the trail
which the Frenchman marked out for them. They
had progressed not more than three hundred
yards when there came to them for a third time
the hallooing of a voice. With a sharp "hup,
hup," and a low crack of his whip Jean stopped
the dogs.

"The Virgin be praised, but that is luck!" he
exclaimed. "They have turned off into another
trail to the east, M'seur. If they had come on to
that break in the bush where we dragged the
sledge through—" He shrugged his shoulders
with a gasp of relief. "*Sacre*, they would not be
fools enough to pass it without wondering!"

Howland had broken the breech of his revolver
and was replacing the three empty cartridges
with fresh ones.

"There will be no mistake next time," he said,
holding out the weapon. "You were as near your

death a few moments ago as ever before in your life, Croisset—and now for a little plain understanding between us. Until we stopped out there I had some faith in you. Now I have none. I regard you as my worst enemy, and though you are deuced near to your friends I tell you that you were never in a tighter box in your life. If I fail in my mission here, you shall die. If others come along that trail before dark, and run us down, I will kill you. Unless you make it possible for me to see and talk with Meleese I will kill you. Your life hangs on my success; with my failure your death is as certain as the coming of night. I am going to put a bullet through you at the slightest suspicion of treachery. Under the circumstances what do you propose to do?"

"I am glad that you changed your mind, M'seur, and I will not tempt you again. I will do the best that I can," said Jean. Through a narrow break in the tops of the banskian pines a few feathery flakes of snow were falling, and

225

Jean lifted his eyes to the slit of gray sky above them. "Within an hour it will be snowing heavily," he affirmed. "If they do not run across our trail by that time, M'seur, we shall be safe."

He led the way through the forest again, more slowly and with greater caution than before, and whenever he looked over his shoulder he caught the dull gleam of Howland's revolver as it pointed at the hollow of his back.

"The devil, but you make me uncomfortable," he protested. "The hammer is up, too, M'seur!"

"Yes, it is up," said Howland grimly. "And it never leaves your back, Croisset. If the gun should go off accidentally it would bore a hole clean through you."

Half an hour later the Frenchman halted where the banskians climbed the side of a sloping ridge.

"If you could trust me I would ask to go on ahead," whispered Jean. "This ridge shuts in the plain, M'seur, and just over the top of it is an old cabin which has been abandoned for

226

many years. There is not one chance in a thousand of there being any one there, though it is a good fox ridge at this season. From it you may see the light in Meleese's window at night."

He did not stop to watch the effect of his last words, but began picking his way up the ridge with the dogs tugging at his heels. At the top he swung sharply between two huge masses of snow-covered rock, and in the lee of the largest of these, almost entirely sheltered from the drifts piled up by easterly winds, they came suddenly on a small log hut. About it there were no signs of life. With unusual eagerness Jean scanned the surface of the snow, and when he saw that there was trail of neither man nor beast in the unbroken crust a look of relief came into his face.

"*Mon Dieu*, so far I have saved my hide," he grinned. "Now, M'seur, look for yourself and see if Jean Croisset has not kept his word!"

A dozen steps had taken him through a screen of shrub to the opposite slope of the ridge. With outstretched arm he pointed down into the plain, and as Howland's eyes followed its direction he stood throbbing with sudden excitement. Less than a quarter of a mile away, sheltered in a dip of the plain, were three or four log buildings rising black and desolate out of the white waste. One of these buildings was a large structure similar to that in which Howland had been imprisoned, and as he looked a team and sledge appeared from behind one of the cabins and halted close to the wall of the large building. The driver was plainly visible, and to Howland's astonishment he suddenly began to ascend the side of this wall. For the moment Howland had not thought of a stair.

Jean's attitude drew his eyes. The Frenchman had thrust himself half out of the screening bushes and was staring through the telescope of his hands. With an exclamation he turned quickly to the engineer.

"Look, M'seur! Do you see that man climbing the stair? I don't mind telling you that he is

228

the one who hit you over the head on the trail, and also one of those who shut you up in the coyote. Those are his quarters at the post, and possibly he is going up to see Meleese. If you were much of a shot you could settle a score or two from here, M'seur."

The figure had stopped, evidently on a platform midway up the side of the building. He stood for a moment as if scanning the plain between him and the mountain, then disappeared. Howland had not spoken a word, but every nerve in his body tingled strangely.

"You say Meleese—is there?" he questioned hesitatingly. "And he—who is that man, Croisset?"

Jean shrugged his shoulders and drew himself back into the bush, turning leisurely toward the old cabin.

"*Non*, M'seur, I will not tell you that," he protested. "I have brought you to this place. I have pointed out to you the stair that leads to the room where you will find Meleese. You may cut me into ribbons for the ravens, but I will tell you no more!"

Again the threatening fire leaped into Howland's eyes.

"I will trouble you to put your hands behind your back, Croisset," he commanded. "I am going to return a certain compliment of yours by tying your hands with this piece of babeesh, which you used on me. After that—"

"And after that, M'seur—" urged Jean, with a touch of the old taunt in his voice, and stopping with his back to the engineer and his hands behind him. "After that?"

"You will tell me all that I want to know," finished Howland, tightening the thong about his wrists.

He led the way then to the cabin. The door was closed, but opened readily as he put his weight against it. The single room was lighted by a window through which a mass of snow had drifted, and contained nothing more than a rude table built against one of the log walls, three supply boxes that had evidently been employed as stools, and a cracked and rust-eaten sheet-iron stove that had from all appearances long passed into disuse. He motioned the Frenchman to a seat at one end of the table. Without a word he then went outside, securely toggled the leading dog, and returning, closed the door and seated himself at the end of the table opposite Jean.

The light from the open window fell full on Croisset's dark face and shone in a silvery streak along the top of Howland's revolver as the muzzle of it rested casually on a line with the other's breast. There was a menacing click as the engineer drew back the hammer.

"Now, my dear Jean, we're ready to begin the real game," he explained. "Here we are, high and dry, and down there—just far enough away to be out of hearing of this revolver when I shoot—are those we're going to play against. So far I've been completely in the dark. I know of no reason why I shouldn't go down there openly and be welcomed and given a good sup-

per. And yet at the same time I know that my
life wouldn't be worth a tinker's damn if I *did*
go down. You can clear up the whole business,
and that's what you're going to do. When I
understand why I am scheduled to be murdered
on sight I won't be handicapped as I now am.
So go ahead and spiel. If you don't, I'll blow
your head off."

Jean sat unflinching, his lips drawn tightly,
his head set square and defiant.

"You may shoot, M'seur," he said quietly.
"I have sworn on a cross of the Virgin to tell you
no more than I have. You could not torture me
into revealing what you ask."

Slowly Howland raised his revolver.

"Once more, Croisset—will you tell me?"

"*Non*, M'seur—"

A deafening explosion filled the little cabin.
From the lobe of Jean's ear there ran a red
trickle of blood. His face had gone deathly pale.
But even as the bullet had stung him within an
inch of his brain he had not flinched.

"Will you tell me, Croisset?"

This time the black pit of the engineer's revolver centered squarely between the Frenchman's eyes.

"*Non*, M'seur."

The eyes of the two men met over the blue steel. With a cry Howland slowly lowered his weapon.

"Good God, but you're a brave man, Jean Croisset!" he cried. "I'd sooner kill a dozen men that I know than you!"

He rose to his feet and went to the door. There was still but little snow in the air. To the north the horizon was growing black with the early approach of the northern night. With a nervous laugh he returned to Jean.

"Deuce take it if I don't feel like apologizing to you," he exclaimed. "Does your ear hurt?"

"No more than if I had scratched it with a thorn," returned Jean politely. "You are good with the pistol, M'seur."

"I would not profit by killing you—just now,"

mused Howland, seating himself again on the box and resting his chin in the palm of his hand as he looked across at the other. "But that's a pretty good intimation that I'm desperate and mean business, Croisset. We won't quarrel about the things I've asked you. What I'm here for is to see Meleese. Now—how is that to happen?"

"For the life of me I don't know," replied Jean, as calmly as though a bullet had not nipped the edge of his ear a moment before. "There is only one way I can see, M'seur, and that is to wait and watch from this mountain top until Meleese drives out her dogs. She has her own team, and in ordinary seasons frequently goes out alone or with one of the women at the post. *Mon Dieu*, she has had enough sledge-riding of late, and I doubt if she will find pleasure in her dogs for a long time."

"I had planned to use you," said Howland, "but I've lost faith in you. Honestly, Croisset, I believe you would stick me in the back almost as quickly as those murderers down there."

"Not in the back, M'seur," smiled the Frenchman, unmoved. "I have had opportunities to do that. *Non*, since that fight back there I do not believe that I want to kill you."

"But I would be a fool to trust you. Isn't that so?"

"Not if I gave you my word. That is something we do not break up here as you do down among the Wekusko people, and farther south."

"But you murder people for pastime—eh, my dear Jean?"

Croisset shrugged his shoulders without speaking.

"See here, Croisset," said Howland with sudden earnestness, "I'm almost tempted to take a chance with you. Will you go down to the post to-night, in some way gain access to Meleese, and give her a message from me?"

"And the message—what would it be?"

"It would bring Meleese up to this cabin to-night."

"Are you sure, M'seur?"

"I am certain that it would. Will you go?"

"*Non*, M'seur."

"The devil take you!" cried Howland angrily. "If I was not certain that I would need you later I'd garrote you where you sit."

He rose and went to the old stove. It was still capable of holding fire, and as it had grown too dark outside for the smoke to be observed from the post, he proceeded to prepare a supper of hot coffee and meat. Jean watched him in silence, and not until food and drink were on the table did the engineer himself break silence.

"Of course, I'm not going to feed you," he said curtly, "so I'll have to free your hands. But be careful."

He placed his revolver on the table beside him after he had freed Croisset.

"I might assassinate you with a fork!" chuckled the Frenchman softly, his black eyes laughing over his coffee cup. "I drink your health, M'seur, and wish you happiness!"

"You lie!" snapped Howland.

Jean lowered the cup without drinking.

"It's the truth, M'seur," he insisted. "Since that *bee*-utiful fight back there I can not help but wish you happiness. I drink also to the happiness of Meleese, also to the happiness of those who tried to kill you on the trail and at the coyote. But, *Mon Dieu*, how is it all to come? Those at the post are happy because they believe that you are dead. You will not be happy until they are dead. And Meleese—how will all this bring happiness to her? I tell you that I am as deep in trouble as you, M'seur Howland. May the Virgin strike me dead if I'm not!"

He drank, his eyes darkening gloomily. In that moment there flashed into Howland's mind a memory of the battle that Jean had fought for him on the Great North Trail.

"You nearly killed one of them—that night —at Prince Albert," he said slowly. "I can't understand why you fought for me then and won't help me now. But you did. And you're afraid to go down there—"

"Until I have regrown a beard," interrupted Jean with a low chuckling laugh. "You would not be the only one to die if they saw me again like this. But that is enough, M'seur. I will say no more."

"I really don't want to make you uncomfortable. Jean," Howland apologized, as he secured the Frenchman's hands again after they had satisfied their hearty appetites, "but unless you swear by your Virgin or something else that you will make no attempt to call assistance I shall have to gag you. What do you say?"

"I will make no outcry, M'seur. I give you my word for that."

With another length of babeesh Howland tied his companion's legs.

"I'm going to investigate a little," he explained. "I am not afraid of your voice, for if you begin to shout I will hear you first. But with your legs free you might take it into your head to run away."

"Would you mind spreading a blanket on the

238

floor, M'seur? If you are gone long this box will grow hard and sharp."

A few minutes later, after he had made his prisoner as comfortable as possible in the cabin, Howland went again through the fringe of scrub bush to the edge of the ridge. Below him the plain was lost in the gloom of night. He could see nothing of the buildings at the post but two or three lights gleaming faintly through the darkness. Overhead there were no stars; thickening snow shut out what illumination there might have been in the north, and even as he stood looking into the desolation to the west the snow fell faster and the lights grew fainter and fainter until all was a chaos of blackness.

In these moments a desire that was almost madness swept over him. Since his fight with Jean the swift passing of events had confined his thoughts to their one objective—the finding of Meleese and her people. He had assured himself that his every move was to be a cool and calculating one, that nothing—not even his great love—should urge him beyond that reason which had made him a master-builder among men. As he stood with the snow falling heavily on him he knew that his trail would be covered before another day—that for an indefinite period he might safely wait and watch for Meleese on the mountain top. And yet, slowly, he made his way down the side of the ridge. A little way out there in the gloom, barely beyond the call of his voice, was the girl for whom he was willing to sacrifice all that he had ever achieved in life. With each step the desire in him grew—the impulse to bring himself nearer to her, to steal across the plain, to approach in the silent smother of the storm until he could look on the light which Jean Croisset had told him would gleam from her window.

He descended to the foot of the ridge and headed into the plain, taking the caution to bury his feet deep in the snow that he might have a trail to guide him back to the cabin. At first he found himself impeded by low bush. Then the plain became more open, and he knew that there was nothing but the night and the snow to shut out his vision ahead. Still he had no motive, no reason for what he did. The snow would cover his tracks before morning. There would be no harm done, and he might get a glimpse of the light, of *her* light.

It came on his vision with a suddenness that set his heart leaping. A dog barked ahead of him, so near that he stopped in his tracks, and then suddenly there shot through the snow-gloom the bright gleam of a lamp. Before he had taken another breath he was aware of what had happened. A curtain had been drawn aside in the chaos ahead. He was almost on the walls of the post—and the light gleamed from high up, from the head of the stair!

For a space he stood still, listening and watching. There was no other light, no other sound after the barking of the dog. About him the snow fell with fluttering noiselessness and it filled him with a sensation of safety. The sharpest eyes could not see him, the keenest ears could not hear him—and he advanced again until before him there rose out of the gloom a huge shadowy mass that was blacker than the night itself. The one lighted window was plainly visible now, its curtain two-thirds drawn, and as he looked a shadow passed over it. Was it a woman's shadow? The window darkened as the figure within came nearer to it, and Howland stood with clenched hands and wildly beating heart, almost ready to call out softly a name. A little nearer—one more step—and he would know. He might throw a chunk of snow-crust, a cartridge from his belt—and then—

The shadow disappeared. Dimly Howland made out the snow-covered stair, and he went to it and looked up. Ten feet above him the light shone out.

He looked into the gloom behind him, into the gloom out of which he had come. Nothing—nothing but the storm. Swiftly he mounted the stair.

CHAPTER XV

FLATTENING himself closely against the black logs of the wall Howland paused on the platform at the top of the stair. His groping hand touched the jam of a door and he held his breath when his fingers incautiously rattled the steel of a latch. In another moment he passed on, three paces—four—along the platform, at last sinking on his knees in the snow, close under the window, his eyes searched the lighted room an inch at a time. He saw a section of wall at first, dimly illuminated; then a small table near the window covered with books and magazines, and beside it a reclining chair buried thick under a great white bear robe. On the table, but beyond his vision, was the lamp. He drew himself a few inches more through the snow, leaning still farther ahead, until he saw

243

the foot of a white bed. A little more and he stopped, his white face close to the window-pane.

On the bed, facing him, sat Meleese. Her chin was buried in the cup of her hands, and he noticed that she was in a dressing-gown and that her beautiful hair was loosed and flowing in glistening waves about her, as though she had just brushed it for the night. A movement, a slight shifting of her eyes, and she would have seen him.

He was filled with an almost mastering impulse to press his face closer, to tap on the window, to draw her eyes to him, but even as his hand rose to do the bidding of that impulse something restrained him. Slowly the girl lifted her head, and he was thrilled to find that another impulse drew him back until his ghostly face was a part of the elusive snow-gloom. He watched her as she turned from him and threw back the glory of her hair until it half hid her in a mass of copper and gold; from his distance he still gazed at her, choking and undecided, while she

gathered it in three heavy strands and plaited
it into a shining braid.

For an instant his eyes wandered. Beyond
her presence the room was empty. He saw a door,
and observed that it opened into another room,
which in turn could be entered through the platform door behind him. With his old exactness
for detail he leaped to definite conclusion. These
were Meleese's apartments at the post, separated
from all others—and Meleese was preparing to
retire for the night. If the outer door was not
locked, and he entered, what danger could there
be of interruption? It was late. The post was
asleep. He had seen no light but that in the window through which he was staring.

The thought was scarcely born before he was
at the platform door. The latch clicked gently
under his fingers; cautiously he pushed the door
inward and thrust in his head and shoulders.
The air inside was cold and frosty. He reached
out an arm to the right and his hand encountered
the rough-hewn surface of a wall; he advanced

245

a step and reached out to the left. There, too, his hand touched a wall. He was in a narrow corridor. Ahead of him there shone a thin ray of light from under the door that opened into Meleese's room. Nerving himself for the last move, he went boldly to the door, knocked lightly to give some warning of his presence, and entered. Meleese was gone. He closed the door behind him, scarce believing his eyes. Then at the far end of the room he saw a curtain, undulating slightly as if from the movement of a person on the other side of it.

"Meleese!" he called softly.

White and dripping with snow, his face bloodless in the tense excitement of the moment, he stood with his arms half reaching out when the curtain was thrust aside and the girl stood before him. At first she did not recognize him in his ghostly storm-covered disguise. But before the startled cry that was on her lips found utterance the fear that had blanched her face gave place to a swift sweeping flood of color. For a space there was no word between them as they stood separated by the breadth of the room, Howland with his arms held out to her in pleading silence, Meleese with her hands clutched to her bosom, her throat atremble with strange sobbing notes that made no more sound than the fluttering of a bird's wing.

And Howland, as he came across the room to her, found no words to say—none of the things that he had meant to whisper to her, but drew her to him and crushed her close to his breast, knowing that in this moment nothing could tell her more eloquently than the throbbing of his own heart, the passionate pressure of his face to her face, of his great love which seemed to stir into life the very silence that encompassed them.

It was a silence broken after a moment by a short choking cry, the quick-breathing terror of a face turned suddenly up to him robbed of its flush and quivering with a fear that still found no voice in words. He felt the girl's arms straining against him for freedom; her eyes were filled with a staring, questioning horror, as though his presence had grown into a thing of which she was afraid. The change was tonic to him. This was what he had expected—the first terror at his presence, the struggle against his will, and there surged back over him the forces he had reserved for this moment. He opened his arms and Meleese slipped from them, her hands clutched again in the clinging drapery of her bosom.

"I have come for you, Meleese," he said as calmly as though his arrival had been expected. "Jean is my prisoner. I forced him to drive me to the old cabin up on the mountain, and he is waiting there with the dogs. We will start back to-night—*now*." Suddenly he sprang to her again, his voice breaking in a low pleading cry. "My God, don't you see now how I love you?" he went on, taking her white face between his two hands. "Don't you understand, Meleese? Jean and I have fought—he is bound hand and foot up there in the cabin—and I am waiting for you—for you—" He pressed her face against

248

him, her lips so close that he could feel their quavering breath. "I have come to fight for you—if you won't go," he whispered tensely. "I don't know why your people have tried to kill me, I don't know why they want to kill me, and it makes no difference to me now. I want you. I've wanted you since that first glimpse of your face through the window, since the fight on the trail—every minute, every hour, and I won't give you up as long as I'm alive. If you won't go with me—if you won't go now—to-night—" He held her closer, his voice trembling in her hair. "If you won't go—I'm going to stay with you!"

There was a thrillingly decisive note in his last words, a note that carried with it more than all he had said before, and as Meleese partly drew away from him again she gave a sharp cry of protest.

"No—no—no—" she panted, her hands clutching at his arm. "You must go back now —now—" She pushed him toward the door, and

249

as he backed a step, looking down into her face, he saw the choking tremble of her white throat, heard again the fluttering terror in her breath. "They will kill you if they find you here," she urged. "They think you are dead—that you fell through the ice and were drowned. If you don't believe me, if you don't believe that I can never go with you, tell Jean—"

Her words seemed to choke her as she struggled to finish.

"Tell Jean what?" he questioned softly.

"Will you go—then?" she cried with sobbing eagerness, as if he already understood her. "Will you go back if Jean tells you everything—everything about me—about—"

"No," he interrupted.

"If you only knew—then you would go back, and never see me again. You would understand—"

"I will never understand," he interrupted again. "I say that it is you who do not understand, Meleese! I don't care what Jean would

250

tell me. Nothing that has ever happened can make me not want you. Don't you understand? Nothing, I say—nothing that has happened—that can ever happen—unless—"

For a moment he stopped, looking straight into her eyes.

"Nothing—nothing in the world, Meleese," he repeated almost in a whisper, "unless you did not tell me the truth back on the trail at Wekusko when you said that it was not a sin to love you."

"And if I tell you—if I confess that it is a sin, that I lied back there—then will you go?" she demanded quickly.

Her eyes flamed on him with a strange light.

"No," he said calmly. "I would not believe you."

"But it is the truth. I lied—lied terribly to you. I have sinned even more terribly, and—and you must go. Don't you understand me now? If some one should come—and find you here—"

"There would be a fight," he said grimly. "I have come prepared to fight." He waited a moment, and in the silence the brown head in front of him dropped slowly and he saw a tremor pass through the slender form, as if it had been torn by an instant's pain. The pallor had gone from Howland's face. The mute surrender in the bowed head, the soft sobbing notes that he heard now in the girl's breath, the confession that he read in her voiceless grief set his heart leaping, and again he drew her close into his arms and turned her face up to his own. There was no resistance now, no words, no pleading for him to go; but in her eyes he saw the prayerful entreaty with which she had come to him on the Wekusko trail, and in the quivering red mouth the same torture and love and half-surrender that had burned themselves into his soul there. Love, triumph, undying faith shone in his eyes, and he crushed her face closer until the lovely mouth lay pouted like a crimson rose for him to kiss.

IN THE BEDROOM CHAMBER

"You—you told me something that wasn't true—once—back there," he whispered, "and you promised that you wouldn't do it again. You haven't sinned—in the way that I mean, and in the way that you want me to believe." His arms tightened still more about her, and his voice was suddenly filled with a tense quick eagerness. "Why don't you tell me everything?" he asked. "You believe that if I knew certain things I would never want to see you again, that I would go back into the South. You have told me that. Then—if you want me to go—why don't you reveal these things to me? If you can't do that, go with me to-night. We will go anywhere—to the ends of the earth—"

He stopped at the look that had come into her face. Her eyes were turned to the window. He saw them filled with a strange terror, and involuntarily his own followed them to where the storm was beating softly against the window-pane. Close to the lighted glass was pressed a man's face. He caught a flashing glimpse of a pair of eyes staring in at them, of a thick, wild beard whitened by the snow. He knew the face. When life seemed slipping out of his throat he had looked up into it that night of the ambush on the Great North Trail. There was the same hatred, the same demoniac fierceness in it now.

With a quick movement Howland sprang away from the girl and leveled his revolver to where the face had been. Over the shining barrel he saw only the taunting emptiness of the storm. Scarcely had the face disappeared when there came the loud shout of a man, the hoarse calling of a name, and then of another, and after that the quick, furious opening of the outer door.

Howland whirled, his weapon pointing to the only entrance. The girl was ahead of him and with a warning cry he swung the muzzle of his gun upward. In a moment she had pushed the bolt that locked the room from the inside, and had leaped back to him, her face white, her breath breaking in fear. She spoke no word, but with a moan of terror caught him by the

arm and pulled him past the light and beyond
the thick curtain that had hidden her when he
had entered the room a few minutes before.
They were in a second room, palely lighted by a
mass of coals gleaming through the open door
of a box stove, and with a second window looking out into the thick night. Fiercely she
dragged him to this window, her fingers biting
deep into the flesh of his arm.

"You must go—through this!" she cried
chokingly. "Quick! O, my God, won't you
hurry? Won't you go?"

Howland had stopped. From the blackness of
the corridor there came the beat of heavy fists
on the door and the rage of a thundering voice
demanding admittance. From out in the night
it was answered by the sharp barking of a dog
and the shout of a second voice.

"Why should I go?" he asked. "I told you a
few moments ago that I had come prepared to
fight, Meleese. I shall stay—and fight!"

"Please—please go!" she sobbed, striving to

pull him nearer to the window. "You can get away in the storm. The snow will cover your trail. If you stay they will kill you—kill you—"

"I prefer to fight and be killed rather than to run away without you," he interrupted. "If you will go—"

She crushed herself against his breast.

"I can't go—now—this way—" she urged. "But I will come to you. I promise that—I will come to you." For an instant her hands clasped his face. "Will you go—if I promise you that?"

"You swear that you will follow me—that you will come down to the Wekusko? My God, are you telling me the truth, Meleese?"

"Yes, yes, I will come to you—if you go now." She broke from him and he heard her fumbling at the window. "I will come—I will come—but not to Wekusko. They will follow you there. Go back to Prince Albert—to the hotel where I looked at you through the window. I will come there—sometime—as soon as I can—"

A blast of cold air swept into his face. He

had thrust his revolver into its holster and now again for an instant he held Meleese close in his arms.

"You will be my wife?" he whispered.

He felt her throbbing against him. Suddenly her arms tightened around his neck.

"Yes, if you want me then—if you want me after you know what I am. Now, go—please, please go!"

He pulled himself through the window, hanging for a last moment to the ledge.

"If you fail to come—within a month—I shall return," he said.

Her hands were at his face again. Once more, as on the trail at Le Pas, he felt the sweet pressure of her lips.

"I will come," she whispered.

Her hands thrust him back and he was forced to drop to the snow below. Scarcely had his feet touched when there sounded the fierce yelp of a dog close to him, and as he darted away into the smother of the storm the brute followed

257

at his heels, barking excitedly in the manner of the mongrel curs that had found their way up from the South. Between the dog's alarm and the loud outcry of men there was barely time in which to draw a breath. From the stair platform came a rapid fusillade of rifle shots that sang through the air above Howland's head, and mingled with the fire was a hoarse voice urging on the cur that followed within a leap of his heels.

The presence of the dog filled the engineer with a fear that he had not anticipated. Not for an instant did the brute give slack to his tongue as they raced through the night, and Howland knew now that the storm and the darkness were of little avail in his race for life. There was but one chance, and he determined to take it. Gradually he slackened his pace, drawing and cocking his revolver; then he turned suddenly to confront the yelping Nemesis behind him. Three times he fired in quick succession at a moving blot in the snow-gloom, and there went up from that blot a wailing cry that he knew was caused by the deep bite of lead.

Again he plunged on, a muffled shout of defiance on his lips. Never had the fire of battle raged in his veins as now. Back in the window, listening in terror, praying for him, was Meleese. The knowledge that she was there, that at last he had won her and was fighting for her, stirred him with a joy that was next to madness. Nothing could stop him now. He loaded his revolver as he ran, slackening his pace as he covered greater distance, for he knew that in the storm his trail could be followed scarcely faster than a walk.

He gave no thought to Jean Croisset, bound hand and foot in the little cabin on the mountain. Even as he had clung to the window for that last moment it had occurred to him that it would be folly to return to the Frenchman. Meleese had promised to come to him, and he believed her, and for that reason Jean was no longer of use to him. Alone he would lose him

self in that wilderness, alone work his way into
the South, trusting to his revolver for food, and
to his compass and the matches in his pocket for
life. There would be no sledge-trail for his
enemies to follow, no treachery to fear. It would
take a thousand men to find him after the night's
storm had covered up his retreat, and if one
should find him they two would be alone to fight
it out.

For a moment he stopped to listen and stare
futilely into the blackness behind him. When
he turned to go on his heart stood still. A
shadow had loomed out of the night half a dozen
paces ahead of him, and before he could raise
his revolver the shadow was lightened by a sharp
flash of fire. Howland staggered back, his
fingers loosening their grip on his pistol, and
as he crumpled down into the snow he heard over
him the hoarse voice that had urged on the dog.
After that there was a space of silence, of black
chaos in which he neither reasoned nor lived, and
then there came to him faintly the sound of other

voices. Finally all of them were lost in one—a moaning, sobbing voice that was calling his name again and again, a voice that seemed to reach to him from out of an infinity of distance, and that he knew was the voice of Meleese. He strove to speak, to lift his arms, but his tongue was as lead, his arms as though fettered with steel bands.

The voice died away. He lived through a cycle of speechless, painless night into which finally a gleam of dawn returned. He felt as if years were passing in his efforts to move, to lift himself out of chaos. But at last he won. His eyes opened, he raised himself. His first sensation was that he was no longer in the snow and that the storm was not beating into his face. Instead there encompassed him a damp dungeon-like chill. Everywhere there was blackness—everywhere except in one spot, where a little yellow eye of fire watched him and blinked at him. At first he thought that the eye must be miles and miles away. But it came quickly nearer—

and still nearer—until at last he knew that it was a candle burning with the silence of a death taper a yard or two beyond his feet.

CHAPTER XVI

IT was the candle-light that dragged Howland quickly back into consciousness and pain. He knew that he was no longer in the snow. His fingers dug into damp earth as he made an effort to raise himself, and with that effort it seemed as though a red-hot knife had cleft him from the top of his skull to his chest. The agony of that instant's pain drew a sharp cry from him and he clutched both hands to his head, waiting and fearing. It did not come again and he sat up. A hundred candles danced and blinked before him like so many taunting eyes and turned him dizzy with a sickening nausea. One by one the lights faded away after that until there was left only the steady glow of the real candle.

The fingers of Howland's right hand were sticky when he drew them away from his head, and he shivered. The tongue of flame leaping out of the night, the thunderous report, the deluge of fire that had filled his brain, all bore their meaning for him now. It had been a close call, so close that shivering chills ran up and down his spine as he struggled little by little to lift himself to his knees. His enemy's shot had grazed his head. A quarter of an inch more, an eighth of an inch even, and there would have been no awakening. He closed his eyes for a few moments, and when he opened them his vision had gained distance. About him he made out indistinctly the black encompassing walls of his prison.

It seemed an interminable time before he could rise and stand on his feet and reach the candle. Slowly he felt his way along the wall until he came to a low, heavy door, barred from the outside, and just beyond this door he found a narrow aperture cut through the decaying logs. It was a yard in length and barely wide enough for him to thrust through an arm.

Three more of these narrow slits in his prison walls he found before he came back again to the door. They reminded him of the hole through which he had looked out on the plague-stricken cabin at the *Maison de Mort Rouge,* and he guessed that through them came what little fresh air found its way into the dungeon.

Near the table on which he replaced the candle was a stool, and he sat down. Carefully he went through his pockets. His belt and revolver were gone. He had been stripped of letters and papers. Not so much as a match had been left him by his captors.

He stopped in his search and listened. Faintly there came to him the ticking of his watch. He felt in his watch pocket. It was empty. Again he listened. This time he was sure that the sound came from his feet and he lowered the candle until the light of it glistened on something yellow an arm's distance away. It was his watch, and close beside it lay his leather wallet. What money he had carried in the pocketbook was untouched, but his personal cards and half a dozen papers that it had contained were gone.

He looked at the time. The hour hand pointed to four. Was it possible that he had been unconscious for more than six hours? He had left Jean on the mountain top soon after nightfall— it was not later than nine o'clock when he had seen Meleese. Seven hours! Again he lifted his hands to his head. His hair was stiff and matted with blood. It had congealed thickly on his cheek and neck and had soaked the top of his coat. He had bled a great deal, so much that he wondered he was alive, and yet during those hours his captors had given him no assistance, had not even bound a cloth about his head.

Did they believe that the shot had killed him, that he was already dead when they flung him into the dungeon? Or was this only one other instance of the barbaric brutishness of those who so insistently sought his life? The fighting blood rose in him with returning strength. If they had left him a weapon, even the small knife they had taken from his pocket, he would still make an effort to settle a last score or two. But now he was helpless.

There was, however, a ray of hope in the possibility that they believed him dead. If they who had flung him into the dungeon believed this, then he was safe for several hours. No one would come for his body until broad day, and possibly not until the following night, when a grave could be dug and he could be carried out with some secrecy. In that time, if he could escape from his prison, he would be well on his way to the Wekusko. He had no doubt that Jean was still a prisoner on the mountain top. The dogs and sledge were there and both rifles were where he had concealed them. It would be a hard race—a running fight perhaps—but he would win, and after a time Meleese would come to him, away down at the little hotel on the Saskatchewan.

He rose to his feet, his blood growing warm, his eyes shining in the candle-light. The thought of the girl as she had come to him out

267

in the night put back into him all of his old fighting strength, all of his unconquerable hope and confidence. She had followed him when the dog yelped at his heels, as the first shots had been fired; she had knelt beside him in the snow as he lay bleeding at the feet of his enemies. He had heard her voice calling to him, had felt the thrilling touch of her arms, the terror and love of her lips as she thought him dying. She had given herself to him; and she would come to him —his lady of the snows—if he could escape.

He went to the door and shoved against it with his shoulder. It was immovable. Again he thrust his hand and arm through the first of the narrow ventilating apertures. The wood with which his fingers came in contact was rotting from moisture and age and he found that he could tear out handfuls of it. He fell to work, digging with the fierce eagerness of an animal. At the rate the soft pulpy wood gave way he could win his freedom long before the earliest risers at the post were awake.

A sound stopped him, a hollow cough from out of the blackness beyond the dungeon wall. It was followed an instant later by a gleam of light and Howland darted quickly back to the table. He heard the slipping of a bolt outside the door and it flashed on him then that he should have thrown himself back into his old position on the floor. It was too late for this action now. The door swung open and a shaft of light shot into the chamber. For a space Howland was blinded by it and it was not until the bearer of the lamp had advanced half-way to the table that he recognized his visitor as Jean Croisset. The Frenchman's face was wild and haggard. His eyes gleamed red and bloodshot as he stared at the engineer.

"*Mon Dieu*, I had hoped to find you dead," he whispered huskily.

He reached up to hang the big oil lamp he carried to a hook in the log ceiling, and Howland sat amazed at the expression on his face. Jean's great eyes gleamed like living coals from out of a death-mask. Either fear or pain had wrought deep lines in his face. His hands trembled as he steadied the lamp. The few hours that had passed since Howland had left him a prisoner on the mountain top had transformed him into an old man. Even his shoulders were hunched forward with an air of weakness and despair as he turned from the lamp to the engineer.

"I had hoped to find you dead, M'seur," he repeated in a voice so low it could not have been heard beyond the door. "That is why I did not bind your wound and give you water when they turned you over to my care. I wanted you to bleed to death. It would have been easier—for both of us."

From under the table he drew forth a second stool and sat down opposite Howland. The two men stared at each other over the sputtering remnant of the candle. Before the engineer had recovered from his astonishment at the sudden appearance of the man whom he believed to be

270

safely imprisoned in the old cabin, Croisset's shifting eyes fell on the mass of torn wood under the aperture.

"Too late, M'seur," he said meaningly. "They are waiting up there now. It is impossible for you to escape."

"That is what I thought about you," replied Howland, forcing himself to speak coolly. "How did you manage it?"

"They came up to free me soon after they got you, M'seur. I am grateful to you for thinking of me, for if you had not told them I might have stayed there and starved like a beast in a trap."

"It was Meleese," said Howland. "I told her."

Jean dropped his head in his hands.

"I have just come from Meleese," he whispered softly. "She sends you her love, M'seur, and tells you not to give up hope. The great God, if she only knew—if she only knew what is about to happen! No one has told her. She is a prisoner in her room, and after that—after that out on the plain—when she came to you and

271

fought like one gone mad to save you—they will not give her freedom until all is over. What time is it, M'seur?"

A clammy chill passed over Howland as he read the time.

"Half-past four."

The Frenchman shivered; his fingers clasped and unclasped nervously as he leaned nearer his companion.

"The Virgin bear me witness that I wish I might strike ten years off my life and give you freedom," he breathed quickly. "I would do it this instant, M'seur. I would help you to escape if it were in any way possible. But they are in the room at the head of the stair—waiting. At six—"

Something seemed to choke him and he stopped.

"At six—what then?" urged Howland. "My God, man, what makes you look so? What is to happen at six?"

Jean stiffened. A flash of the old fire gleamed

in his eyes, and his voice was steady and clear when he spoke again.

"I have no time to lose in further talk like this, M'seur," he said almost harshly. "They know now that it was I who fought for you and for Meleese on the Great North Trail. They know that it is I who saved you at Wekusko. Meleese can no more save me than she can save you, and to make my task a little harder they have made me their messenger, and—"

Again he stopped, choking for words.

"What?" insisted Howland, leaning toward him, his face as white as the tallow in the little dish on the table.

"Their executioner, M'seur."

With his hands gripped tightly on the table in front of him Jack Howland sat as rigid as though an electric shock had passed through him.

"Great God!" he gasped.

"First I am to tell you a story, M'seur," continued Croisset, leveling his reddened eyes to the engineer's. "It will not be long, and I pray the Virgin to make you understand it as we people of the North understand it. It begins sixteen years ago."

"I shall understand, Jean," whispered Howland. "Go on."

"It was at one of the company's posts that it happened," Jean began, "and the story has to do with Le M'seur, the Factor, and his wife, *L'Ange Blanc*—that is what she was called, M'seur—the White Angel. *Mon Dieu*, how we loved her! Not with a wicked love, M'seur, but with something very near to that which we give our Blessed Virgin. And our love was but a pitiful thing when compared with the love of these two, each for the other. She was beautiful, gloriously beautiful as we know women up in the big snows; like Meleese, who was the youngest of their children.

"Ours was the happiest post in all this great northland, M'seur," continued Croisset after a moment's pause; "and it was all because of this woman and the man, but mostly because of the woman. And when the little Meleese came—she was the first white girl baby that any of us had ever seen—our love for these two became something that I fear was almost a sacrilege to our dear Lady of God. Perhaps you can not understand such a love, M'seur; I know that it can not be understood down in that world which you call civilization, for I have been there and have seen. We would have died for the little Meleese, and the other Meleese, her mother. And also, M'seur, we would have killed our own brothers had they as much as spoken a word against them or cast at the mother even as much as a look which was not the purest. That is how we loved her sixteen years ago this winter, M'seur, and that is how we love her memory still."

"She is dead," uttered Howland, forgetting in these tense moments the significance Jean's story might hold for him.

"Yes; she is dead. M'seur, shall I tell you how she died?"

Croisset sprang to his feet, his eyes flashing,

275

his lithe body twitching like a wolf's as he stood for an instant half leaning over the engineer.

"Shall I tell you how she died, M'seur?" he repeated, falling back on his stool, his long arms stretched over the table. "It happened like this, sixteen years ago, when the little Meleese was four years old and the oldest of the three sons was fourteen. That winter a man and his boy came up from Churchill. He had letters from the Factor at the Bay, and our Factor and his wife opened their doors to him and to his son, and gave them all that it was in their power to give.

"*Mon Dieu*, this man was from that glorious civilization of yours, M'seur—from that land to the south where they say that Christ's temples stand on every four corners, but he could not understand the strange God and the strange laws of our people! For months he had been away from the companionship of women, and in this great wilderness the Factor's wife came into his life as the flower blossoms in the desert. Ah, M'seur, I can see now how his wicked heart strove to accomplish the things, and how he failed because the glory of our womanhood up here has come straight down from Heaven. And in failing he went mad—mad with that passion of the race I have seen in Montreal, and then—ah, the Great God, M'seur, do you not understand what happened next?"

Croisset lifted his head, his face twisted in a torture that was half grief, half madness, and stared at Howland, with quivering nostrils and heaving chest. In his companion's face he saw only a dead white pallor of waiting, of half comprehension. He leaned over the table again, controlling himself by a mighty effort.

"It was at that time when most of us were out among the trappers, just before our big spring caribou roast, when the forest people came in with their furs, M'seur. The post was almost deserted. Do you understand? The woman was alone in her cabin with the little Meleese—and when we came back at night she was dead. Yes, M'seur, she killed herself, leaving a few written words to the Factor telling him what had happened.

"The man and the boy escaped on a sledge after the crime. *Mon Dieu*, how the forest people leaped in pursuit! Runners carried the word over the mountains and through the swamps, and a hundred sledge parties searched the forest trails for the man-fiend and his son. It was the Factor himself and his youngest boy who found them, far out on the Churchill trail. And what happened then, M'seur? Just this: While the man-fiend urged on his dogs the son fired back with a rifle, and one of his bullets went straight through the heart of the pursuing Factor, so that in the space of one day and one night the little Meleese was made both motherless and fatherless by these two whom the devil had sent to destroy the most beautiful thing we have ever known in this North. Ah, M'seur, you turn white! Does it bring a vision to you now? Do you hear the crack of that rifle? Can you see—"

"My God!" gasped Howland. Even now he

278

understood nothing of what this tragedy might mean to him—forgot everything but that he was listening to the terrible tragedy that had come to the woman who was the mother of the girl he loved. He half rose from his seat as Croisset paused; his eyes glittered, his death-white face was set in tense fierce lines, his finger-nails dug into the board table, as he demanded, "What happened then, Croisset?"

Jean was eying him like an animal. His voice was low.

"They escaped, M'seur."

With a deep breath Howland sank back. In a moment he leaned again toward Jean as he saw come into the Frenchman's eyes a slumbering fire that a few seconds later blazed into vengeful malignity when he drew slowly from an inside pocket of his coat a small parcel wrapped and tied in soft buckskin.

"They have sent you this, M'seur," he said. " 'At the very last,' they told me, 'let him read this.' "

With his eyes on the parcel, scarcely breathing, Howland waited while with exasperating slowness Croisset's brown fingers untied the cord that secured it.

"First you must understand what this meant to us in the North, M'seur," said Jean, his hands covering the parcel after he had finished with the cord. "We are different who live up here—different from those who live in Montreal, and beyond. With us a lifetime is not too long to spend in avenging a cruel wrong. It is our honor of the North. I was fifteen then, and had been fostered by the Factor and his wife since the day my mother died of the smallpox and I dragged myself into the post, almost dead of starvation. So it happened that I was like a brother to Meleese and the other three. The years passed, and the desire for vengeance grew in us as we became older, until it was the one thing that we most desired in life, even filling the gentle heart of Meleese, whom we sent to school in Montreal when she was eleven, M'seur. It was three years later

—while she was still in Montreal—that I went on one of my wandering searches to a post at the head of the Great Slave, and there, M'seur— there—"

Croisset had risen. His long arms were stretched high, his head thrown back, his up- turned face aflame with a passion that was al- most that of prayer.

"M'seur, I thank the great God in Heaven that it was given to Jean Croisset to meet one of those whom we had pledged our lives to find—and I slew him!"

He stood silent, eyes partly closed, still as if in prayer. When he sank into his chair again the look of hatred had gone from his face.

"It was the father, and I killed him, M'seur— killed him slowly, telling him of what he had done as I choked the life from him; and then, a little at a time, I let the life back into him, forcing him to tell me where I would find his son, the slayer of Meleese's father. And after that I closed on his throat until he was dead, and my dogs dragged his body through three hundred miles of snow that the others might look on him and know that he was dead. That was six years ago, M'seur."

Howland was scarcely breathing.

"And the other—the son—" he whispered tensely. "You found him, Croisset? You killed him?"

"What would you have done, M'seur?"

Howland's hands gripped those that guarded the little parcel.

"I would have killed him, Jean."

He spoke slowly, deliberately.

"I would have killed him," he repeated.

"I am glad of that, M'seur."

Jean was unwrapping the buckskin, fold after fold of it, until at last there was revealed a roll of paper, soiled and yellow along the edges.

"These pages are taken from the day-book at the post where the woman lived," he explained softly, smoothing them under his hands. "Each day the Factor of a post keeps a reckoning of incidents as they pass, as I have heard that sea captains do on shipboard. It has been a company law for hundreds of years. We have kept these pages to ourselves, M'seur. They tell of what happened at our post sixteen years ago this winter."

As he spoke the half-breed came to Howland's side, smoothing the first page on the table in front of him, his slim forefinger pointing to the first few lines.

"They came on this day," he said, his breath close to the engineer's ear. "These are their names, M'seur—the names of the two who destroyed the paradise that our Blessed Lady gave to us many years ago."

In an instant Howland had read the lines. His blood seemed to dry in his veins and his heart to stand still. For these were the words he read: "On this day there came to our post, from the Churchill way, John Howland and his son."

With a sharp cry he sprang to his feet, overturning the stool, facing Croisset, his hands clenched, his body bent as if about to spring.

Jean stood calmly, his white teeth agleam. Then, slowly, he stretched out a hand.

"M'seur John Howland, will you read what happened to the father and mother of the little Meleese sixteen years ago? Will you read, and understand why your life was sought on the Great North Trail, why you were placed on a case of dynamite in the Wekusko coyote, and why, with the coming of this morning's dawn— at six—"

He paused, shivering. Howland seemed not to notice the tremendous effort Croisset was making to control himself. With the dazed speechlessness of one recovering from a sudden blow he turned to the table and bent over the papers that the Frenchman had laid out before him. Five minutes later he raised his head. His face was as white as chalk. Deep lines had settled about his mouth. As a sick man might, he lifted his hand and passed it over his face and through his hair. But his eyes were afire. Involuntarily Jean's body gathered itself as if to meet attack.

"I have read it," he said huskily, as though the speaking of the words caused him a great effort. "I understand now. My name is John Howland. And my father's name was John Howland. I understand."

There was silence, in which the eyes of the two men met.

"I understand," repeated the engineer, advancing a step. "And you, Jean Croisset—do you believe that I am *that* John Howland—the John Howland—the son who—"

He stopped, waiting for Jean to comprehend, to speak.

"M'seur, it makes no difference what I believe now. I have but one other thing to tell you here —and one thing to give to you," replied Jean. "Those who have tried to kill you are the three brothers. Meleese is their sister. Ours is a strange country, M'seur, governed since the beginning of our time by laws which we have made ourselves. To those who are waiting above no torture is too great for you. They have condemned you to death. This morning, exactly as the minute hand of your watch counts off the hour of six, you will be shot to death through one of these holes in the dungeon walls. And this—this note from Meleese—is the last thing I have to give you."

He dropped a folded bit of paper on the table. Mechanically Howland reached for it. Stunned and speechless, cold with the horror of his death sentence, he smoothed out the note. There were only a few words, apparently written in great haste.

"I have been praying for you all night. If God fails to answer my prayers I will still do as I have promised—and follow you.

"MELEESE."

He heard a movement and lifted his eyes. Jean was gone. The door was swinging slowly inward. He heard the wooden bolt slip into place, and after that there was not even the sound of a moccasined foot stealing through the outer darkness.

CHAPTER XVII

FOR many minutes Howland stood waiting as if life had left him. His eyes were on the door, but unseeing. He made no sound, no movement again toward the aperture in the wall. Fate had dealt him the final blow, and when at last he roused himself from its first terrible effect there remained no glimmering of hope in his breast, no thought of the battle he had been making for freedom a short time before. The note fluttered from his fingers and he drew his watch from his pocket and placed it on the table. It was a quarter after five. There still remained forty-five minutes.

Three-quarters of an hour and then—death! There was no doubt in his mind this time. Even in the coyote, with eternity staring him in the face, he had hoped and fought for life. But here

287

there was no hope, there was to be no fighting. Through one of the black holes in the wall he was to be shot down, with no chance to defend himself, to prove himself innocent. And Meleese— did she, too, believe him guilty of that crime?

He groaned aloud, and picked up the note again. Softly he repeated her last words to him: "If God fails to answer my prayers I will still do as I have promised, and follow you." Those words seemed to cry aloud his doom. Even Meleese had given up hope. And yet, was there not a deeper significance in her words? He started as if some one had struck him, his eyes agleam.

" 'I will follow you.' "

He almost sobbed the words this time. His hands trembled and he dropped the paper again on the table and turned his eyes in staring horror toward the door. What did she mean? Would Meleese kill herself if he was murdered by her brothers? He could see no other meaning in her last message to him, and for a time after the chilling significance of her words struck his heart he scarce restrained himself from calling aloud for Jean. If he could but send a word back to her, tell her once more of his great love—that the winning of that love was ample reward for all that he had lost and was about to lose, and that it gave him such happiness as he had never known even in this last hour of his torture!

Twice he shouted for Croisset, but there came no response save the hollow echoings of his own voice in the subterranean chambers. After that he began to think more sanely. If Meleese was a prisoner in her room it was probable that Croisset, who was now fully recognized as a traitor at the post, could no longer gain access to her. In some secret way Meleese had contrived to give him the note, and he had performed his last mission for her.

In Howland's breast there grew slowly a feeling of sympathy for the Frenchman. Much that he had not understood was clear to him now. He understood why Meleese had not revealed the names of his assailants at Prince Albert and We-

kusko; he understood why she had fled from him
after his abduction, and why Jean had so faith-
fully kept secrecy for her sake. She had fought
to save him from her own flesh and blood, and
Jean had fought to save him, and in these last
minutes of his life he would liked to have had
Croisset with him that he might have taken his
hand and thanked him for what he had done.
And because he had fought for him and Meleese
the Frenchman's fate was to be almost as terrible
as his own. It was he who would fire the fatal
shot at six o'clock. Not the brothers, but Jean
Croisset, would be his executioner and murderer.

The minutes passed swiftly, and as they went
Howland was astonished to find how coolly he
awaited the end. He even began to debate with
himself as to through which hole the fatal shot
would be fired. No matter where he stood he was
in the light of the big hanging lamp. There was
no obscure or shadowy corner in which for a few
moments he might elude his executioner. He
even smiled when the thought occurred to him

that it was possible to extinguish the light and crawl under the table, thus gaining a momentary delay. But what would that delay avail him? He was anxious for the fatal minute to arrive, and be over.

There were moments of happiness when in the damp horror of his death-chamber there came before him visions of Meleese, grown even sweeter and more lovable, now that he knew how she had sacrificed herself between two great loves —the love of her own people and the love of himself. And at last she had surrendered to him. Was it possible that she could have made that surrender if she, like her brothers, believed him to be the murderer of her father—the son of the man-fiend who had robbed her of a mother? It was impossible, he told himself. She did not believe him guilty. And yet—why had she not given him some such word in her last message to him?

His eyes traveled to the note on the table and he began searching in his coat pockets. In one of them he found the worn stub of a pencil, and for many minutes after that he was oblivious to the passing of time as he wrote his last words to Meleese. When he had finished he folded the paper and placed it under his watch. At the final moment, before the shot was fired, he would ask Jean to take it. His eyes fell on his watch dial and a cry burst from his lips.

It lacked but ten minutes of the final hour!

Above him he heard faintly the sharp barking of dogs, the hollow sound of men's voices. A moment later there came to him an echo as of swiftly tramping feet, and after that silence.

"Jean," he called tensely. "Ho, Jean—Jean Croisset—"

He caught up the paper and ran from one black opening to another, calling the Frenchman's name.

"As you love your God, Jean, as you have a hope of Heaven, take this note to Meleese!" he pleaded. "Jean—Jean Croisset—"

There came no answer, no movement outside,

and Howland stilled the beating of his heart to listen. Surely Croisset was there! He looked again at the watch he held in his hand. In four minutes the shot would be fired. A cold sweat bathed his face. He tried to cry out again, but something rose in his throat and choked him until his voice was only a gasp. He sprang back to the table and placed the note once more under the watch. Two minutes! One and a half! One!

With a sudden fearless cry he sprang into the very center of his prison, and flung out his arms with his face to the hole next the door. This time his voice was almost a shout.

"Jean Croisset, there is a note under my watch on the table. After you have killed me take it to Meleese. If you fail I shall haunt you to your grave!"

Still no sound—no gleam of steel pointing at him through the black aperture. Would the shot come from behind?

Tick—tick—tick—tick—

He counted the beating of his watch up to

twenty. A sound stopped him then, and he closed his eyes, and a great shiver passed through his body.

It was the tiny bell of his watch tinkling off the hour of six!

Scarcely had that sound ceased to ring in his brain when from far through the darkness beyond the wall of his prison there came a creaking noise, as if a heavy door had been swung slowly on its hinges, or a trap opened—then voices, low, quick, excited voices, the hurrying tread of feet, a flash of light shooting through the gloom. They were coming! After all it was not to be a private affair, and Jean was to do his killing as the hangman's job is done in civilization—before a crowd. Howland's arms dropped to his side. This was more terrible than the other—this seeing and hearing of preparation, in which he fancied that he heard the click of Croisset's gun as he lifted the hammer.

Instead it was a hand fumbling at the door. There were no voices now, only a strange moaning sound that he could not account for. In another moment it was made clear to him. The door swung open, and the white-robed figure of Meleese sprang toward him with a cry that echoed through the dungeon chambers. What happened then—the passing of white faces beyond the doorway, the subdued murmur of voices, were all lost to Howland in the knowledge that at the last moment they had let her come to him, that he held her in his arms, and that she was crushing her face to his breast and sobbing things to him which he could not understand. Once or twice in his life he had wondered if realities might not be dreams, and the thought came to him now when he felt the warmth of her hands, her face, her hair, and then the passionate pressure of her lips on his own. He lifted his eyes, and in the doorway he saw Jean Croisset, and behind him a wild, bearded face—the face that had been over him when life was almost choked from him on the Great North Trail. And beyond these two he saw still others, shining ghostly and indistinct in

the deeper gloom of the outer darkness. He
strained Meleese to him, and when he looked down
into her face he saw her beautiful eyes flooded
with tears, and yet shining with a great joy. Her
lips trembled as she struggled to speak. Then
suddenly she broke from his arms and ran to
the door, and Jean Croisset came between them,
with the wild bearded man still staring over his
shoulder.

"M'seur, will you come with us?" said Jean.

The bearded man dropped back into the thick
gloom, and without speaking Howland followed
Croisset, his eyes on the shadowy form of Meleese. The ghostly faces turned from the light,
and the tread of their retreating feet marked the
passage through the blackness. Jean fell back
beside Howland, the huge bulk of the bearded
man three paces ahead. A dozen steps more and
they came to a stair down which a light shone.
The Frenchman's hand fell detainingly on
Howland's arm, and when a moment later they
reached the top of the stairs all had disappeared

but Jean and the bearded man. Dawn was breaking, and a pale light fell through the two windows of the room they had entered. On a table burned a lamp, and near the table were several chairs. To one of these Croisset motioned the engineer, and as Howland sat down the bearded man turned slowly and passed through a door. Jean shrugged his shoulders as the other disappeared.

"*Mon Dieu*, that means that he leaves it all to me," he exclaimed. "I don't wonder that it is hard for him to talk, M'seur. Perhaps you have begun to understand!"

"Yes, a little," replied Howland. His heart was throbbing as if he had just finished climbing a long hill. "That was the man who tried to kill me. But Meleese—the—" He could go no further. Scarce breathing, he waited for Jean to speak.

"It is Pierre Thoreau," he said, "eldest brother to Meleese. It is he who should say what I am about to tell you, M'seur. But he is too full of

297

grief to speak. You wonder at that? And yet I tell you that a man with a better soul than Pierre Thoreau never lived, though three times he has tried to kill you. Do you remember what you asked me a short time ago, M'seur—if I thought that *you* were the John Howland who murdered the father of Meleese sixteen years ago? God's saints, and I did until hardly more than half an hour ago, when some one came from the South and exploded a mine under our feet. It was the youngest of the three brothers. M'seur we have made a great mistake, and we ask your forgiveness."

In the silence the eyes of the two men met across the table. To Howland it was not the thought that his life was saved that came with the greatest force, but the thought of Meleese, the knowledge that in that hour when all seemed to be lost she was nearer to him than ever. He leaned half over the table, his hands clenched, his eyes blazing. Jean did not understand, for he went on quickly.

"I know it is hard, M'seur. Perhaps it will be impossible for you to forgive a thing like this. We have tried to kill you—kill you by a slow torture, as we thought you deserved. But think for a moment, M'seur, of what happened up here sixteen years ago this winter. I have told you how I choked life from the man-fiend. So I would have choked life from you if it had not been for Meleese. I, too, am guilty. Only six years ago we knew that the right John Howland—the son of the man I slew—was in Montreal, and we sent to seek him this youngest brother, for he had been a long time at school with Meleese and knew the ways of the South better than the others. But he failed to find him at that time, and it was only a short while ago that this brother located you.

"As Our Blessed Lady is my witness, M'seur, it is not strange that he should have taken you for the man we sought, for it is singular that you bear him out like a brother in looks, as I remember the boy. It is true that François made a

299

great error when he sent word to his brothers suggesting that if either Gregson or Thorne was put out of the way you would probably be sent into the North. I swear by the Virgin that Meleese knew nothing of this, M'seur. She knew nothing of the schemes by which her brothers drove Gregson and Thorne back into the South. They did not wish to kill them, and yet it was necessary to do something that you might replace one of them, M'seur. They did not make a move alone but that something happened. Gregson lost a finger. Thorne was badly hurt—as you know. Bullets came through their window at night. With Jackpine in their employ it was easy to work on them, and it was not long before they sent down asking for another man to replace them."

For the first time a surge of anger swept through Howland.

"The cowards!" he exclaimed. "A pretty pair, Croisset—to crawl out from under a trap to let another in at the top!"

"Perhaps not so bad as that," said Jean. "They were given to understand that they—and they alone—were not wanted in the country. It may be that they did not think harm would come to you, and so kept quiet about what had happened. It may be, too, that they did not like to have it known that they were running away from danger. Is not that human, M'seur? Anyway, you were detailed to come, and not until then did Meleese know of all that had occurred."

The Frenchman stopped for a moment. The glare had faded from Howland's eyes. The tense lines in his face relaxed.

"I—I—believe I understand everything now, Jean," he said. "You traced the wrong John Howland, that's all. I love Meleese, Jean. I would kill John Howland for her. I want to meet her brothers and shake their hands. I don't blame them. They're men. But, somehow, it hurts to think of her—of Meleese—as—as almost a murderer."

"*Mon Dieu*, M'seur, has she not saved your

301

life! Listen to this! It was then—when she knew what had happened—that Meleese came to me—whom she had made the happiest man in the world because it was she who brought my Mariane over from Churchill on a visit especially that I might see her and fall in love with her, M'seur—which I did. Meleese came to me—to Jean Croisset—and instead of planning your murder, M'seur, she schemed to save your life—with me—who would have cut you into bits no larger than my finger and fed you to the carrion ravens, who would have choked the life out of you until your eyes bulged in death, as I choked that one up on the Great Slave! Do you understand, M'seur? It was Meleese who came and pleaded with me to save your life—before you had left Chicago, before she had heard more of you than your name, before—"

Croisset hesitated, and stopped.

"Before what, Jean?"

"Before she had learned to love you, M'seur."

"God bless her!" exclaimed Howland.

"You believe this, M'seur?"

"As I believe in a God."

"Then I will tell you what she did, M'seur," he continued in a low voice. "The plan of the brothers was to make you a prisoner near Prince Albert and bring you north. I knew what was to happen then. It was to be a beautiful vengeance, M'seur—a slow torturing death on the spot where the crime was committed sixteen years ago. But Meleese knew nothing of this. She was made to believe that up here, where the mother and father died, you would be given over to the proper law—to the mounted police who come this way now and then. She is only a girl, M'seur, easily made to believe strange things in such matters as these, else she would have wondered why you were not given to the officers in Prince Albert. It was the eldest brother who thought of her as a lure to bring you out of the town into their hands, and not until the last moment, when they were ready to leave for the South, did she over-hear words that aroused her suspicions that they were about to kill you. It was then, M'seur, that she came to me."

"And you, Jean?"

"On the day that Mariane promised to become my wife, M'seur, I promised in Our Blessed Lady's name to repay my debt to Meleese, and the manner of payment came in this fashion. Jackpine, too, was her slave, and so we worked together. Two hours after Meleese and her brothers had left for the South I was following them, shaven of beard and so changed that I was not recognized in the fight on the Great North Trail. Meleese thought that her brothers would make you a prisoner that night without harming you. Her brothers told her how to bring you to their camp. She knew nothing of the ambush until they leaped on you from cover. Not until after the fight, when in their rage at your escape the brothers told her that they had intended to kill you, did she realize fully what she had done. That is all, M'seur. You know what happened after that. She dared not tell you at Prekuske

304

who your enemies were, for those enemies were of her own flesh and blood, and dearer to her than life. She was between two great loves, M'seur—the love for her brothers and—"

Again Jean hesitated.

"And her love for me," finished Howland.

"Yes, her love for you, M'seur."

The two men rose from the table, and for a moment stood with clasped hands in the smoky light of lamp and dawn. In that moment neither heard a tap at the door leading to the room beyond, nor saw the door move gently inward, and Meleese, hesitating, framed in the opening.

It was Howland who spoke first.

"I thank God that all these things have happened, Jean," he said earnestly. "I am glad that for a time you took me for that other John Howland, and that Pierre Thoreau and his brothers schemed to kill me at Prince Albert and Wekusko, for if these things had not occurred as they have I would never have seen Meleese. And now, Jean—"

His ears caught sound of movement, and he turned in time to see Meleese slipping quietly out

"Meleese!" he called softly. "Meleese!"

In an instant he had darted after her, leaving Jean beside the table. Beyond the door there was only the breaking gloom of the gray morning, but it was enough for him to see faintly the figure of the girl he loved, half turned, half waiting for him. With a cry of joy he sprang forward and gathered her close in his arms.

"Meleese—my Meleese—" he whispered.

After that there came no sound from the dawn-lit room beyond, but Jean Croisset, still standing by the table, murmured softly to himself: "Our Blessed Lady be praised, for it is all as Jean Croisset would have it—and now I can go to my Mariane!"

THE END

JAMES OLIVER CURWOOD'S
STORIES OF ADVENTURE

A GENTLEMAN OF COURAGE

THE ALASKAN

THE COUNTRY BEYOND

THE FLAMING FOREST

THE VALLEY OF SILENT MEN

THE RIVER'S END

THE GOLDEN SNARE

NOMADS OF THE NORTH

KAZAN

BAREE, SON OF KAZAN

THE COURAGE OF CAPTAIN PLUM

THE DANGER TRAIL

THE HUNTED WOMAN

THE FLOWER OF THE NORTH

THE GRIZZLY KING

ISOBEL

THE WOLF HUNTERS

THE GOLD HUNTERS

THE COURAGE OF MARGE O'DOONE

BACK TO GOD'S COUNTRY

GROSSET & DUNLAP, *Publishers,* NEW YORK

ZANE GREY'S NOVELS

TAPPAN'S BURRO
THE VANISHING AMERICAN
THE THUNDERING HERD
THE CALL OF THE CANYON
WANDERER OF THE WASTELAND
TO THE LAST MAN
THE MYSTERIOUS RIDER
THE MAN OF THE FOREST
THE DESERT OF WHEAT
THE U. P. TRAIL
WILDFIRE
THE BORDER LEGION
THE RAINBOW TRAIL
THE HERITAGE OF THE DESERT
RIDERS OF THE PURPLE SAGE
THE LIGHT OF WESTERN STARS
THE LAST OF THE PLAINSMEN
THE LONE STAR RANGER
DESERT GOLD
BETTY ZANE
THE DAY OF THE BEAST

*   *   *   *   *   *

LAST OF THE GREAT SCOUTS
The life story of "Buffalo Bill" by his sister Helen Cody Wetmore, with Foreword and conclusion by Zane Grey.

ZANE GREY'S BOOKS FOR BOYS

ROPING LIONS IN THE GRAND CANYON
KEN WARD IN THE JUNGLE
THE YOUNG LION HUNTER
THE YOUNG FORESTER
THE YOUNG PITCHER
THE SHORT STOP
THE RED-HEADED OUTFIELD AND OTHER
BASEBALL STORIES

GROSSET & DUNLAP, *Publishers*, NEW YORK

EDGAR RICE BURROUGH'S NOVELS

May be had wherever books are sold. Ask for Grosset & Dunlap's list.

THE MAD KING

THE MOON MAID

THE ETERNAL LOVER

BANDIT OF HELL'S BEND, THE

CAVE GIRL, THE

LAND THAT TIME FORGOT, THE

TARZAN OF THE APES

TARZAN AND THE JEWELS OF OPAR

TARZAN AND THE ANT MEN

TARZAN THE TERRIBLE

TARZAN THE UNTAMED

BEASTS OF TARZAN, THE

RETURN OF TARZAN, THE

SON OF TARZAN, THE

JUNGLE TALES OF TARZAN

AT THE EARTH'S CORE

PELLUCIDAR

THE MUCKER

A PRINCESS OF MARS

GODS OF MARS, THE

WARLORD OF MARS, THE

THUVIA, MAID OF MARS

CHESSMEN OF MARS, THE

GROSSET & DUNLAP, *Publishers*, NEW YORK

RAFAEL SABATINI'S NOVELS

Jesi, a diminutive city of the Italian Marches, was the birth-place of Rafael Sabatini, and here he spent his early youth. The city is glamorous with those centuries the author makes live again in his novels with all their violence and beauty.

Mr. Sabatini first went to school in Switzerland and from there to Lycee of Oporto, Portugal, and like Joseph Conrad, he has never attended an English school. But English is hardly an adopted language for him, as he learned it from his mother, an English woman who married the Maestro-Cavaliere Vincenzo Sabatini.

Today Rafael Sabatini is regarded as "The Alexandre Dumas of Modern Fiction."

MISTRESS WILDING

A romance of the days of Monmouth's rebellion. The action is rapid, its style is spirited, and its plot is convincing.

FORTUNE'S FOOL

All who enjoyed the lurid lights of the French Revolution with Scaramouche, or the brilliant buccaneering days of Peter Blood, or the adventures of the Sea-Hawk, the corsair, will now welcome with delight a turn in Restoration London with the always masterful Col. Randall Holles.

BARDELYS THE MAGNIFICENT

An absorbing story of love and adventure in France of the early seventeenth century.

THE SNARE

It is a story in which fact and fiction are delightfully blended and one that is entertaining in high degree from first to last.

CAPTAIN BLOOD

The story has glamor and beauty, and it is told with an easy confidence. As for Blood himself, he is a superman, compounded of a sardonic humor, cold nerves, and hot temper. Both the story and the man are masterpieces. A great figure, a great epoch, a great story.

THE SEA-HAWK

"The Sea-Hawk" is a book of fierce bright color and amazing adventure through which stalks one of the truly great and masterful figures of romance.

SCARAMOUCHE

Never will the reader forget the sardonic Scaramouche, who fights equally well with tongue and rapier, who was "born with the gift of laughter and a sense that the world was mad."

GROSSET & DUNLAP, *Publishers*, NEW YORK